I0602296

# THE STRAWBERRY GIRL

## A HULI INTERGALACTIC STORY

### LEAH R CUTTER

KNOTTED ROAD PRESS

**The Strawberry Girl**
Copyright © 2020 Leah Cutter
All rights reserved
Published by Knotted Road Press
www.KnottedRoadPress.com

ISBN: 978-1-64470-122-5

Cover Art:

ID 140286785 © Chainat | Dreamstime.com
ID 128685547 © Vitaliy Lesik | Dreamstime.com
ID 52628760 © Elena Polina | Dreamstime.com

Cover and interior design copyright © 2020 Knotted Road Press

http://www.KnottedRoadPress.com

**Come someplace new...**
Are you a traveler? Do you enjoy exploring strange new worlds, new
cultures, new people?

Journey into the various lands envisioned by Leah Cutter.

Sign up for my newsletter and I'll start you on your travels with a free copy
of my book, *The Island Sampler*.

I will never spam you or use your email for nefarious purposes. You can
also unsubscribe at any time.

http://www.LeahCutter.com/newsletter/

**The Shadow Wars Trilogy**

*The Raven and the Dancing Tiger*

*The Guardian Hound*

*War Among the Crocodiles*

**The Clockwork Fairy Kingdom**

*The Clockwork Fairy Kingdom*

*The Maker, the Teacher, and the Monster*

*The Dwarven Wars*

**The Chronicles of Franklin**

*Franklin Versus The Popcorn Thief*

*Franklin Versus The Soul Thief*

*Franklin Versus The Child Thief*

**Contemporary Fantasy**

*Siren's Call*

*The Immortals' War*

# PART ONE
# THE RULE OF LAW

# ONE

REN STOOD on her raft and slowly paddled across the still bay. The sun had just barely risen, painting the sky beautiful shades of blue and pink. To her right, the mainland and the waking city of New Hong Kong spread out like a fan. It felt to her as if the city hung in limbo, poised but not yet leaping into action, as the day shift workers weren't yet on their way to the factories and the night shift was still winding down. Though factory workers made up the majority of the city, Ren wasn't one of them and had very few friends who were.

To Ren's left flowed the open bay and the two hundred or so *shaoshu* islands, those places where she felt she could breathe. The air that morning carried just a hint of the vast sea beyond Baohu Bay, the familiar feeling of salt tingling the back of her throat, welcoming her. The drone of cars and the buzzing of neon lights washed out as she crossed over the water, growing fainter until she could no longer hear anything but the soft sound of her paddle entering and leaving the water.

A streak of white split the peaceful sky—the morning shuttle taking workers up to the orbiting factories, where they made special metals and strange organics, out of the clutches of gravity. They'd work there for ten days, then return back to Jung Wa, staying planetside for ten days, generally sleeping and enjoying themselves before their next shift.

The five-by-ten-foot raft Ren stood on only looked as though it was made out of old-fashioned wood. The front of it was a rectangle, while Ren stood on a tongue in the back, so she could easily reach the water on either side of her. A small mat of woven reeds made out of native *luwei* plants cushioned her feet and aided the illusion of an older craft.

However, each board of the raft was composed of an unbreakable plastic tube that wouldn't corrode or attract the native barnacles. *Huli* Transport—the company she worked for—actually owned it, along with her paddle and the uniform she wore, a long-sleeved dark brown jumpsuit that was waterproof as well as breathable.

Ren sometimes felt as though the company also owned her soul and merely leased it to her. Maybe someday she'd earn enough to buy it back.

While Ren steered the raft with her paddle, as well as moved it some, she actually used a slight current of magic to sail across the waves. The distances she was required to travel were too great for her to get there by paddling alone. Not unless she wanted to spend all day at it.

Ren wore her thick black hair unlike anyone else. She'd cut it spacer short on the left side, while leaving it hanging long, down to her jawline, on the right side. She generally wore it as a curtain over her right eye, primarily to hide her right cheek and the bright red birthmark there. As a child, she'd been teased, called "strawberry girl." The perfect people in New Hong Kong wanted nothing to do with her, thinking she was bad luck. The normal remedies for restoring skin hadn't worked on Ren. There was something wrong with her genes. Every time her parents had saved enough for the treatment to remove the mark, it would grow back a month later.

Fortunately, the routine tests that all children on civilized worlds took also showed that Ren had some level of magical ability. Unfortunately, it wasn't enough to get her off planet and up to the stars, working for *Huli* Transport on one of the spaceships that traveled the vast distances between planets via portals, wizards, and magic.

While Ren still worked for the company, she was stuck here, on the planet of Jung Wa where she'd been born, delivering messages between humans, the alien natives, and the gods, as well as transporting such individuals between the islands.

Ren breathed in the morning air and pushed her hair back, hooking it behind her ear, using both of her eyes to watch the still waters of the bay, enjoying the colors playing across the sky. Spring had just arrived, with beautiful blooming flowers available in the markets and springing up in many gardens. While the sun would get warm during the day, the nights were still cool. It wouldn't get really warm for another month or so.

Graceful gulls winged their way across the water, catching insects as they flew. Of course, they weren't really gulls, and certainly not Earth gulls, but they were close enough that it didn't really matter. Same with the herons and cranes that nested in the *luwei* reeds close to shore, the large tuna and yellowtail fish caught by the local fishermen, and even the butterflies and mosquitoes who delighted and plagued the people who'd migrated to the planet. The colonists had brought their terms for things, and their dependents continued the tradition, regardless of the fact that the Seidaren—the natives to the planet—had their own names for everything.

Ren used steady strokes to help move herself across the bay. She knew from experience that it would take her about thirty minutes to cross from the city to the first of the southern islands, known as Butterfly Land.

Though Seidaren had had a different name for their island, they'd been so amused by the name the humans had come up with they'd adopted it.

The island was a long, soft curve of land, maybe ten miles stretching from north to south, but only four miles wide. The land itself was hilly, with undisturbed native forests nestled in a band running through the center of it. Great flocks of butterflies lived there, the adults bright blue and the size of Ren's hand. They pollinated the trees and the rest of the crops in the region, as this planet didn't have the equivalent of bees.

Cliffs made up the northern and southern tips of the island, so all the marinas, quays, and docks were located in the center part. The public piers closest to the mainland on the eastern side of the island were larger, made out of steel and plastic, and could accommodate the engine-powered ferries that carried passengers to and from the islands. The public piers on the far side of the island, away from the mainland, were much smaller and crafted from native wood that frequently had to be replaced.

Ren's first passenger that morning was Hanshu, a regular, who she ferried to and from the main city at least once a week. He waited for her at the first pier on the western side of the island, waving and smiling as she paddled closer. She shook her head and let her hair hang down before she approached. While she didn't believe that Hanshu would be repulsed by her birthmark, it was just habit.

No one but family got to see her full face, and even they didn't see it often.

Ren wasn't certain what Hanshu was. He appeared to be a human wizard whom the natives had allowed to live on one

6

of their islands. While Ren had enough magical ability to sense power in others, Hanshu's magic always appeared to be muffled, as if he had a shade pulled down over his light. In addition, she'd never forget the first time she'd dropped him off at the main pier in New Hong Kong, and all those around him had seemed startled to see him, as if they hadn't noticed him until he was on top of them.

That was usually the mark of a god, or at least a very powerful hero or immortal. While mundanes knew about magic, they couldn't see it or interact with it. Gods walked among them, invisible to all but those with the strongest magic.

"Good morning! Good morning!" Hanshu called cheerfully as Ren maneuvered the raft next to the pier. He wore a typical shift worker's outfit that day—a navy blue jumpsuit with a colorful red-and-white polka-dot scarf and a matching hat with a broad brim. It must be some sort of disguise. Hanshu did not work in a factory, and normally wore very nice suits. Maybe he had a consultation with one though, and had dressed this way to put whoever he was meeting with at ease.

"Good morning, sir," Ren said, holding the raft steady as Hanshu jumped down onto it lightly.

Some of Ren's passengers needed help stepping from a pier to the raft. She was tall for a woman—close to six feet—and had developed strong muscles from hours of paddling, so she occasionally carried beings from the raft to the pier or vice versa. Some passengers used magic to aid themselves, floating through the air. There were only a few who could jump down like Hanshu, landing perfectly in the center of her raft and not rocking it in the least.

"Would you care for a seat, sir?" Ren asked. She carried both chairs as well as benches folded up in the compartments under her mat.

"I'll stand. Thank you," Hanshu said.

"Very good, sir," Ren said as she turned the raft around.

"Beautiful morning, isn't it?" Hanshu said as they passed the northern tip of the island and started heading directly toward the mainland.

"Yes, sir," Ren said. She spoke clearly, distinctly. She made a point of never mumbling. While she might hide her looks, she didn't have to hide her voice.

"What news do you carry from the city today?" Hanshu asked.

Ren couldn't help but smile. Some of her passengers wanted to talk during their trips. Others needed pure silence, the kind that came from being on the water. Seemed that Hanshu was in a talkative mood today.

"The new spaceport has been delayed. Again," Ren said.

Hanshu gave a sharp whistle. "What happened this time?"

"Some of the special electronics got corroded en route. *Huli* is charging the carrier with negligence. The carrier is claiming that the parts weren't good in the first place."

Magic and electronics didn't co-exist peacefully, as Ren had learned from personal experience. She regularly fried the circuits on the cheap wristwatch phones that everyone wore. Instead, she had to carry a separate device that she kept in a special case that was both waterproof as well as magic-proof. It was similar to an ancient pager. She could receive messages on it, but then she had to find a terminal in order to call back. Fortunately, terminals were scattered throughout the city and at the piers of the bigger islands, as factory workers frequently had the same sort of setup: electronics weren't allowed in certain parts of the factories.

Hanshu nodded. "*Huli* will win," he said softly. "The carrier should just acknowledge their loss and move on."

Ren shrugged. While she worked for the same company,

she didn't have the level of devotion as most of the messengers. Or most of the people on the planet, for that matter. She figured it was just her faulty wiring, the same bad genes that marred her face.

While there were still local governments, *Huli* Transport was the only universe-wide governing body. They exercised their control economically: if a planet didn't abide by the conventions set down, they were likely to be cut off from all trade. No one really committed wars anymore as a result, since *Huli* Transport viewed them as bad for business.

"What else have you heard?" Hanshu said. He stayed facing forward, watching the city approaching.

A loud horn blared to Ren's right before she could reply —a ferry making its way to the islands. It could carry over a hundred passengers on its two decks, and frequently did. Ren used her magic and pushed hard on her raft to stay out of the path of the ferry. It was running early this morning, as normally Ren didn't cross the ferry until her second or third trip out for the day.

She glanced at the large boat. No, that wasn't the regular ferry, but a special one, used to carry Important People.

Whoever it was that the ferry was picking up must have a very high rank, as they appeared to rate an entire boat all to themselves.

At least only the ferry's horn was loud. The ferry's engine was electric. It buzzed softly as it traveled, the waves against the bow frequently drowning out the sound.

Ren still hated the ferries. She'd blast them all if she were a stronger magician, turn the hulls into ashes and send the flames shooting high. While she couldn't hear the engine, she felt it as it approached, a wave of ants crawling all over her skin. Sometimes, when she got too close, they were like biting ants.

She added more speed to her tiny raft to get out of the

way of the coming miasma, trying to miss the edge of the cloud. It seemed to have worked, as only her back crawled for a few moments when the boat passed behind them, and then it was gone.

"Do you feel the ferry's cloud as well?" Hanshu asked, looking at her from over his shoulder.

Ren wasn't sure if it was better to tell him the truth or to lie. Would it be viewed as a weakness? Or as a sign of strong magical ability?

Finally, she nodded. "I do, sir." She wasn't about to elaborate on how awful the ferries made her feel the few times she'd ridden on one.

"So do I," Hanshu said. "It's why the service you provide is so invaluable," he added.

Huh. Ren had thought that she was the only one who reacted so strongly to the ferries. She knew that no one in her family felt them as she did. They hadn't understood why she'd cried the entire time they'd ridden on one as a special treat to go out to the islands for a day trip, when she'd been a little girl.

"Though I'm not sure why you're merely a messenger if you're that sensitive," Hanshu said, looking at her with an expression of great curiosity. "You need to get tested again.'

Ren didn't know how to reply to that. She was already twenty-nine. Most people who went on to become wizards started their training when they were sixteen or eighteen.

"I'll look into it, sir," Ren finally replied when she realized that Hanshu was waiting for her to say something.

He nodded, seemingly satisfied, and went back to watching the city approaching. She had the sense that he was looking forward to being in the embrace of New Hong Kong again, like a returning lover. But he couldn't stay there, any more than she could. He'd return to his island in a day or at most, a week.

As Ren didn't have another client to pick up right away, she decided to go into the *Huli* Transport messenger office, to see if perhaps there were more training options available to her.

What was the worst that could happen?

# TWO

Aᴛᴛᴇʀ Rᴇɴ ᴅʀᴏᴘᴘᴇᴅ Hanshu off at one of the main piers, watching him startle people as usual as he walked toward them, she turned her craft north, heading toward the *Huli Transport* quay. It was located on the northern side of the grand curve of the port, close to the marina where she lived on a large houseboat with her parents, as her older brothers had already moved away. Not many boats were out on the water at that point—the fishermen were already long gone, and the tourists and businessmen hadn't yet begun their day. Water taxies—smaller than her raft and only able to carry two or three people—clustered together at the end of every public pier, waiting to ferry their first customers of the day, either up the canals of the city or between the islands.

The roar of the city kept up a constant barrage—the whine of scooters, the clanging of bicycle bells, the swoosh of the electric train that ran along the edge of the water. Occasionally, she'd hear the hum of a drone making deliveries.

Ren passed a small boat selling *gua bao* off the side—a soft steamed bun filled with spicy pork belly, cucumber slices, and pickled radishes. It smelled delicious, but she really should wait and have some of the noodles served free to the messengers at the office. That way, maybe she could have a regular dinner and not feel so hungry, as she did most of the time.

The *Huli* Transport quay was short, with only a dozen berths sticking out of either side where a boat could be docked. Small sailing boats took up most of the spaces. They were generally used for pleasure and not for deliveries, for entertaining visiting clients as well as the occasional powerful being.

Though some of the immortals had been born fishermen, they appeared to enjoy going out onto the water and have someone else sail and do all the work.

Up on the quay itself were racks for kayaks and canoes, again for important clients who wanted to be ferried around that way. Ren rarely piloted those other boats, though she'd been trained to use all of them and was annually recertified in their operation.

There was also a rack for the rafts. Ren's raft was only one of three. She always felt a touch of pride when she thought about it, that there weren't as many raft operators as there were of the other crafts. Then again, the rafts mimicked the boats the Seidaren had used in ancient time. They weren't exotic enough for the Important People.

Ren lifted her raft out of the water with her magic, slotting it into its rack and placing her paddle on top. The other two racks were empty—Jiangzhu and Genai must be ferrying their own passengers that morning. There was a friendly competition between the three raft messengers, each trying to pick up the most clients for a week. They all had their regulars, and unless one of them exaggerated greatly, they generally had about the same number each week.

As Ren's raft was the only one being stored, she used a

magical lock to secure the raft to the rack, pressing the palm of her hand against the plastic and envisioning a bubble of blue encasing it. Anyone magical trying to take her raft was in for a severe shock. Someone mundane would see the raft as undesirable, and would walk away.

Ren slowly made her way down the quay. She automatically took deep breaths as she walked, working to calm herself. The breeze from the land carried the smell of burning electric motors and rotting oranges. Blaring music from a kiosk displaying a shampoo ad made her jump. Engines whined and she heard loud, raucous cackling. Though she knew they weren't laughing at her, she still tugged on the hair on her right side, making sure it completely covered her cheek.

At the end of the quay, the company of course had a row of electric scooters that the messengers could use to get themselves around the city. Though Ren could drive one, she was never comfortable doing so. They weren't as bad as the ferries, but that was just a matter of scale and intensity. The biting of the ants would grow stronger the longer she drove around.

Like many workers, Ren wore her ident card on a lanyard around her neck, the card itself tucked in under her jumpsuit so it wouldn't get in her way. It was one of the smaller cards, not much longer than her thumb, with all her information imbedded in its paper-thin form. She tugged it out and pressed her card against the card reader also at the end of the quay, calling one of the company buses to come and get her.

The display on the card reader let her know that there was already a bus en route, and she only had a couple of minutes to wait. Ren tried to get herself to relax. Most people —all right, everyone she knew—enjoyed New Hong Kong, thrived on the energy of the city, being with all the people, going to the shops, listening to the music, trying all the different foods. Ren couldn't stand it. Though it was cheaper for her family to live on a houseboat, part of the reason why her parents had stayed there after they could have afforded an apartment was because Ren couldn't live anywhere else.

If she ever got rich enough, she'd move to one of the smaller islands. Except she'd also have to get permission from the Seidaren to do that. The humans and the natives had a strict arrangement. The Seidaren lived along the coasts, on all the islands, and on the water. Humans were allowed to take over the interior of the small continents. The two races shared the oceans which took up over ninety percent of the planet.

While the Seidaren weren't a space-traveling people and lived only on the one planet of Jung Wa, they were still remarkably advanced. They had floating cities that traversed the waters, traveling from one ocean to the next. None of the humans, or the wizards, were exactly sure how they moved such large masses, the physics being a bit skewed.

The Seidaren appeared humanoid, with the regular count of eyes, ears, arms and legs. They weren't exactly human, though. They had a turquoise tinge to their skin, generally had sandy blond fuzz that almost looked like hair, and the adults tended to be short, between four to five feet tall. Most of the humans who'd settled New Hong Kong were of Asian descent, with black hair and eyes, tanned skin, and a fold at the eyelid. Cantonese was the human tongue they shared.

Ren never saw any of the Seidaren in the city. Occasionally she might pass one of their boats on the water, the pilot always waving at her in a friendly manner. But that was it. Though one of the most popular vids was about the supposed relationship between a human and a Seidaren, very few humans had actually ever seen one or interacted with them. Ren always laughed when she saw ads for the show, and often wondered what types of shows the Seidaren might create about the humans and their blundering ways.

By the time the bus came to pick Ren up, half of the dozen seats were already full. She didn't know any of the people, which wasn't surprising, really. The company employed over ten thousand in New Hong Kong alone, at many different locations, and had both a mundane shipping arm as well as the magical messenger side.

Ren kept her head down as she made her way to an empty seat on the right side of the bus, so her left side was to the other passengers. The cushions were new and soft, much softer than what Ren usually sat on, as she was used to the harder benches in the houseboat. The air smelled stale, as if it had been recycled too many times, all the freshness squeezed out of it. At least the bus was quiet, for now. The company buses were tolerable for Ren, and she could ride one comfortably for an hour or more before the ants would start biting.

As the bus pulled away, Ren let herself look up, away from the window.

The man sitting directly across the aisle stared hard at her.

Ren tugged on her hair out of habit, making sure that it completely covered the cheek turned away from everyone.

Still, the man stared.

What, did he think she was some kind of exotic? She wasn't the only messenger on the bus. She'd seen at least one other brown jumpsuit just two seats back. The man staring at her was dressed as a manager, with a white shirt, black suit, and light blue tie. She didn't bother trying to figure out if he had magic or not. Chances were that if he did, he'd be much stronger than she was. Most everyone was. Plus, his suit was so very expensive. Why was he taking the company bus?

Why hadn't he arranged for private transportation? It must be a face-saving gesture on his part.

Ren turned back to look out the window, doing her best to ignore the rude stranger. Tall buildings with flats above and retail below flashed by. Neon lotus blossoms floated in midair above the sidewalk, opening and closing, as an advertisement for a Buddhist retreat center, the kind that promised great relaxation at an astonishing price. Business workers were starting to take over the streets, walking to their office cubicles. The bus passed packs of factory workers on black bicycles, heading to their shift.

When Ren looked back, the strange man was ignoring her, looking out his own window. She felt his eyes begin to slide in her direction again and quickly looked away.

It couldn't be because he found her attractive. Her strange haircut and prickly attitude quickly discouraged most people. In addition, she was far too old for anyone to be interested in her. She'd long ago accepted the fate her parents expected of her, after the first treatment for her birthmark failed; namely, for her to stay single and take care of them as they aged, while her two older brothers married and started their own families.

Finally, after three other stops, the bus pulled up to the messenger offices. Ren and the other worker in a brown jumpsuit were the only ones to get off.

She felt the eyes of that stranger boring into her as she walked across the sidewalk and into the building.

She hoped that would be the last time she saw the man, but her gut told her that this was far from their last encounter.

# THREE

REN KNOCKED on the open door of her supervisor's office, getting Xiyi's attention.

"Come in, Meiren, come in," the woman said, gesturing for Ren to enter.

Ren couldn't help but grimace. No one but Xiyi used Ren's full name, no matter how many times Ren had corrected the woman. Ren's parents had literally named her "Beautiful Person." Ren had never gotten a straight story from her parents, whether the name had been chosen before or after her birth, before or after they'd seen her ruined face for the first time.

In the end, it didn't really matter. She *hated* her name. She was not beautiful. So she'd shortened it to just Ren, as that part was true. She was a person. Nothing more.

Xiyi wore a nice white blouse with the emblem of *Huli* Transport—a little brown fox—embroidered above her left breast. Her black hair had been curled again recently, and hung in soft waves around her smiling, round face. She cultivated an old-fashioned beauty, with bright white teeth and voluptuous curves, the kind that got men to reminisce about good old days that had never really existed.

"What can I help you with today?" Xiyi asked as she put the tablet she'd been reading to the side.

Ren carefully sat down in one of the guest chairs, obviously made of plastic with cheap gray cushions. Though it looked as if it wouldn't hold her weight, it turned out to be quite stable, if very uncomfortable. While Xiyi might be welcoming in her manner, she didn't actually want the people who came to visit to stay for very long.

Xiyi's desk was immaculate, as always. Though Ren would hate to have to come to an office every day, if she ever was forced to, she would keep it as clean and tidy as Xiyi's. Files were neatly put away in the cabinets behind the woman's desk, a single sumi-e watercolor painting of a waterfall hung from the wall, and a simulated window covered the back wall, showing far away mountains.

"I was wondering if there was any additional testing or magical training that I should have," Ren said.

"Let me check," Xiyi said, pulling her tablet back in front of her. She paused for a moment, looking up Ren's records. "Ah, you're growing more sensitive, aren't you?" she asked after a moment.

"I am," Ren said, surprised that her supervisor might already know that.

"It's in your file," Xiyi said. She expanded something on the screen, then turned the tablet around to show Ren the chart she'd pulled up. "The company predicted that you would grow more sensitive to electronic noise as you grew older."

Ren stiffened. The office suddenly felt much smaller. The air grew thick and hard to breathe. "I see," she said.

The chart showed her sensitivity getting steadily worse, until it became debilitating in a few years.

"Has it gotten bad?" Xiyi asked, solicitous, her concern apparent.

"Not at all, no, it has not," Ren said, shaking her head. She actually hadn't noticed her sensitivities getting stronger. Then again, she rarely exposed herself to most parts of the modern world. Maybe she was much worse and she just didn't know it.

"Then why did you come in to ask about more testing?" Xiyi said, her eyes narrowing.

Crap. Did Xiyi think that Ren could no longer do her job? That she shouldn't be a messenger anymore? According to the chart, it should be at least half a dozen more years until she could no longer work.

"This morning, my passenger, Hanshu, said I should look into getting tested again," Ren quickly explained, placing the blame firmly on him.

Xiyi's eyes grew much larger. "Hanshu?" she asked, clearly surprised.

Ren nodded miserably. She couldn't lose this job. There really wasn't anything else she could do.

"Well, if Hanshu thought you should be retested, then you need to be retested right away," Xiyi said. "Just a moment." She called up something else on her tablet, then held her wrist phone up and began speaking rapidly into it.

Ren sat, stunned. Who was Hanshu? What was he, exactly?

And why did his word carry such weight in the company?

---

REN LEFT the testing room exhausted. Every bit of magical power had been drained from her, and then some. Even the lights in the wide corridor leading to the front entrance seemed dim.

She paused and tried to pull herself together before she pushed out of the wide lobby and back out into the streets of New Hong Kong. It was the middle of the afternoon—she'd been testing since just after lunch. Xiyi had rearranged Ren's schedule and all her clients for the day.

The day was warm and sunny, the air hot and humid. Ren longed for the cool breezes that generally came off the bay. At least it was early enough that the streets weren't full of workers. Ren could walk along the river walk without being overwhelmed by everyone coming and going.

The testing center faced Market Canal—one of four large waterways that snaked through the city. The water looked sluggish to Ren, as if it hadn't been refreshed but instead allowed to sit and grow stagnant. A water taxi hurried by, but even its wake barely stirred the waters along the edges of the canal.

The Seidaren had provided the humans with giant pumps to direct the water through the canals of New Hong Kong, with the understanding that the humans would maintain the pumps as well as keep their waters fresh. Had the one along this canal broken?

Ren walked slowly down the waterway, heading toward the jetty where the company kept water taxis. Only a few other people passed her as she walked, all of them too concerned with their own lives to pay any attention to her. She still felt more vulnerable than usual, probably due to how tired she was. She tugged at her hair, keeping it over her cheek, her protective armor, as it were.

The testing had been both good and bad. Good, in that Ren did have more power than she used to. Not off the charts strong, but still slightly stronger than had been predicted by the company.

Bad, in that Ren had very little control over her power.

In order to do great magical deeds, wizards needed both a tremendous amount of magical power as well as the ability to focus keenly.

The tester had suggested that Ren retake some of the classes that the company offered in order to gain more control and focus. Ren didn't bother explaining that she'd taken all of those classes twice, some of them three times. None of them had helped in the slightest.

Besides, while Ren was stronger than she used to be, she still didn't have enough power to be promoted to a wizard. The best she could hope for would be a low-level manager position, even if she learned more focus.

Thanks but no thanks. She'd stick to being a messenger

Ren wrinkled her nose when she caught a whiff of the water. Gods, no, that was awful. Someone needed to clean that canal. There was no way she was getting into a water taxi and actually traveling across it.

She passed the jetty for the taxies, then turned and walked away from the canal. Just two blocks away was one of the main thoroughfares, Market Street. She could take a bus back to the bay, then either hire a water taxi or transfer to a second bus that would eventually drop her off at the marina where she lived. Though it would take a lot more time to get back home going overland instead of cutting through on one of the canals, she had no choice.

That water hadn't just been stale, but dead.

How had the inspectors let that happen? The city needed its water. People fished out of the waterways, supporting and supplementing their diets, stretching their budgets. It wasn't just her who would be affected by them no longer containing fresh water.

A young woman with three small children waited beside Ren. She seemed too young to have three little ones. The two older ones chased each other around their mother, playing some made-up game. The tall sign that indicated the area was a stop appearing to be "safe" as they couldn't get caught and be made "it" when touching it. The mother held the third child, an infant, to her chest while she read something on her wrist phone, scrolling along and absent-mindedly telling the other children to behave while they continued to race around, loudly giggling and occasionally screeching when one or the other was tagged.

Ren did her best to ignore them, though she wished the mother was paying more attention to her children and less to whatever she was reading.

While Ren didn't know for certain, she'd always thought that she'd be a good mother. She had patience for children, at least for her brothers' kids. They liked playing games with her. The oldest girl always had new made-up stories for Ren every time they came over as well, fantastic tales of dragons and magic. Ren would pick the girl up and they'd dance, the little girl inventing worlds on the fly.

According to the display on the bus stop sign, a bus would be there in ten minutes. Ren knew the bus trackers were generally accurate—only sometimes did a bus get stuck or break down and never actually make it, the display never updating itself.

She breathed a sigh of relief when she saw the sign update itself to nine minutes. There was a chance she could get out of the city before it broke her.

Scooters and motorcycles raced by in the street in front of her, sounding like packs of angry bees. Very few people could afford private cars. The few Ren did see were tiny two-seaters, electric of course, with snub noses and tiny trunks.

"Excuse me, Miss?"

Ren couldn't help but startle, jumping, before she

glanced over her shoulder at the person who'd approached her without her noticing.

It was the same manager that she'd seen that morning, the one on the bus who'd been staring at her.

"You work as a messenger for *Huli* Transport, right?" he asked.

Ren nodded cautiously. Of course she did. She was wearing the uniform of a messenger, and he'd seen her on a company bus.

"Can I talk with you? Just a few minutes. You'll still make your bus," he assured her. "I just have a question."

"All right," Ren said. She didn't see the harm in it. The man wasn't about to attack her, or assault her, not in the middle of the street in broad daylight. Plus, while she still might not be the strongest magically, she still was stronger than most women physically.

He turned and walked up the street, stopping between two shops, next to a glass door that led to flats above the stores.

Ren followed after him, curious. What did the stranger want? Had he been hanging around all day, waiting for her? He certainly looked like Important People, not like someone who would bother with the likes of her. If he had been tracking her movements, he would have had his own people do it, not looking for her himself.

As Ren drew closer, he waved a hand negligently in the air. She felt, rather than saw, the bubble that immediately enclosed them, the sounds of the city abruptly dropping off.

Anyone magical wouldn't be able to listen in on their conversation. Anyone mundane wouldn't just ignore them— they probably wouldn't even notice the pair of them standing there.

Whoever this manager was, he had much more magic than Ren would have expected. She peered closer at the man.

Tiny, subtle blue dots that matched his light-blue tie decorated his shirt, marking it of a much higher quality than she'd first realized. His nails were perfectly manicured, his hands soft, unlike Ren's weather-roughed and paddle-strengthened ones. Though his hair was completely black, Ren would bet it was dyed, as the wrinkles on his face said he was older than he looked. He had a large nose and a small mouth, and his eyes looked sharp and hard.

"I am Wang Guanki," the man said, bowing his head to her.

"Ren," she said in return. She stubbornly crossed her arms over her chest when he gave her a questioning look. She didn't need to give him anything more than a handle to call her by, and certainly not her family name. He was the one who'd wanted to speak with her, not the other way around.

"All right, Ren, how long have you been a messenger for *Huli*?" Mr. Wang asked. He seemed intent on finding out more about her. Couldn't he just search her records or something?

Ren did the math in her head. "Twelve years," she said. "Since I finished high school."

"What wizard do you work with regularly?" Mr. Wang said.

"I don't," Ren said. "I work on the water, with the rafts. I carry passengers mostly, not messages."

Mr. Wang seemed surprised at that. "What, you don't deliver through portals?" he said.

"I don't," Ren said.

Most of the messengers primarily delivered messages to other beings via portals that were created and held by wizards. Ren was one of the few who rarely did portal work.

Being a messenger was very dangerous. Not only could something go wrong with a delivery, there was always the chance that a hitchhiker could catch a ride in a portal, killing not only the messenger but the wizard. By rarely working with portals, Ren knew she would live longer, particularly if she remained a messenger.

"Interesting," Mr. Wang said.

"Why is that?" Ren said. What was it that the manager was looking for?

Instead of answering her, Mr. Wang merely nodded and said, "Thank you for your time." He waved away the barrier that had cut them off from the rest of the city.

The noise came rushing back in, feeling to Ren like a physical assault. She gasped and took a stumbling step backward.

The manager had already vanished. He was probably still walking down the street, but her eyes wouldn't be able to focus on him or find him.

What did this Wang Guanki want from her? Should she tell Xiyi about him?

The bus approached the stop as Ren walked back. She pulled out her ident card, as it also contained her bus pass. She stepped onto the crowded bus, holding onto the rail near the top of the ceiling, no seats available.

She had no idea why Mr. Wang had wanted to speak to her. But he was a manager for *Huli* Transport, as well as a powerful magician. Surely he didn't want to involve her in anything bad.

However, despite slowing her heartrate by meditating hard, Ren couldn't chase away the unease that followed her.

# FOUR

REN TOOK a deep breath as she stepped from the pier and onto the houseboat she shared with her parents.

Home at last.

The front deck of the boat was painted the light gray of happy clouds, the kind that brought good luck. The walls of the house built up from the large hull were painted bright red and orange, with beautiful light blue trim. Because her parents could afford a better place but stayed on the houseboat instead, they took very good care of it, repainting the wood every year, making the house seem so cheery, particularly compared to some of their neighbors who also were moored to pier number nine in the marina.

The houseboat was only twelve feet wide, but it was seventy feet long. Ren walked along the side, all the way to the back of the boat. Though there was a door in the front, it led straight to her parent's bedroom. Behind the bedroom was now a living room, but it had been her brothers' room while Ren was growing up. Just past the living room was a covered causeway between the front and the back of the boat, with doors on either side, one leading to the front of the house, and the other leading directly to the bathroom and kitchen. The hatch to the hull was also there, though there weren't any rooms down below—her family used it for storage and utilities.

At the end of the boat, while the back deck was the width of the boat, it was only a few feet long. Ren would sometimes unfold a chair and look out over the water, past the marina and out onto the bay, particularly as the sun was setting over the city to her right. A ladder led from the back of the boat down to the smaller boats that the family used to get around the marina and other parts of the city. Only Ren's flat skiff was there—her parents used their dinghies to commute to their jobs in the city.

The door to Ren's room was protected both magically and physically. The door hadn't been touched. Ren checked it every time, though there wasn't a high rate of crime in the area.

Ren took a deep breath as she entered her room, taking in the familiar scents of home, the smell of the garlic and chicken congee they'd had for breakfast, mingled with the scent of peppermint, the only plant Ren kept, as she'd never managed to kill it (unlike the lucky bamboo, imported from Earth, that had been wasted on her as she'd managed to turn it brown within days).

Very little covered the light green walls of Ren's room. She had a beautiful sumi-e painting of a pair of red-headed cranes dancing that hung above her bed, just to the left of the door. A quilt made out of hundreds of shades of brown and stitched together with gold-colored thread covered the bed, along with a multitude of pillows in all the colors of the rainbow. Just past the bed was one of two windows, one looking west, while the other faced east. The small wooden armoire she had for her clothes was primarily filled with uniforms, jumpsuits hanging on the one side, shirts with the company logo and sturdy pants neatly folded on the other. While she sometimes thought about buying herself more clothes, she never bothered—she wore her uniform most of the time, and only dressed in something else one day a week.

Ren didn't have a terminal or any other electronics in her room. Her light came from the delicate, hand-painted glass oil lamps she hung from the ceiling, or her own mage light when she didn't want to bother with the lamps. She'd bought extra shielding for the ceiling once she'd started working, then painted it with a glittering white paint. The roof of the houseboat was covered in solar scales and provided all the power they needed for the kitchen, and the rest of the lights, as well as small water jets at the edges of the hull that they could use to maneuver the houseboat. The shielding ensured that Ren could sleep at nights. In addition, she'd bought paint from the company store (at a greatly reduced price for magical employees) that kept her room isolated: any magic that she performed in there wouldn't trickle out and affect the rest of the boat.

The plain wooden floor was covered in the softest rugs Ren could afford, made out of a dark brown spongy material that cushioned her feet. Though Ren had a desk in the far corner, she rarely sat at it, preferring instead to either sit on her bed or to grab a couple of pillows and relax on the floor.

Very little evidence of her primary hobby could be seen. Only the tiny little folded paper flower on the corner of her desk gave it away.

One of the classes that the company regularly taught in order to give their magical employees more focus was origami. While Ren had really taken to the paper folding, she'd never found that it had helped her control her power. She'd continued with her hobby though, and would spend evenings involved in intricate folds and pretty creations.

Without bothering to change clothes, Ren laid down on

her bed and immediately closed her eyes. She was so drained from both the testing as well as the exhausting trip through the city. However, sleep eluded her.

Who was Wang Guanki? For that matter, who was Hanshu? What did they want from her? And what was wrong with Market Canal? Was there anyone she could tell about it? She'd have to remember to ask her parents later.

And speaking of them...She heard the familiar whine of the electric motor of her mom's dinghy pull up. Ren got up and went out onto the back deck to say hi, as well as to help unload the groceries.

Ren was the tallest member of her family; her mom was the next tallest at five feet, ten inches. The pair of them would tease the male members about being short and made for the earth while they'd been made for heaven and the clouds. Ren had also inherited her mom's eyes, at least according to her dad, soft and almond shaped. Her mom wore her hair long. Though she frequently let it hang loose, today she wore it pulled back, braided along the sides of her head then the braids braided together.

Mom was the only one who didn't wear uniforms to work. Instead, she always had on nice blouses that merely looked expensive, with skirts and heels.

"I was hoping you'd be here to help," Mom said as she lifted the first bag, full of oranges.

Ren's schedule constantly changed. While that was something that she really enjoyed, she knew that it sometimes drove her parents crazy, as they could never depend on her being home at any particular time. For example, that morning while she'd gotten up with them before the dawn, there had been a good chance that she wouldn't have returned until well after dinner.

"How was your day?" Ren politely asked as she lifted the bags her mom handed to her.

Mom sold jewelry at one of the high-end stores downtown. She'd only been with the store for seven years, but she'd studied all the aspects of diamonds and other gems that they sold so was valued for her knowledge. In addition, she had had a bit of luck when she'd first started, landing a big client who was a collector, so her commissions had always been good.

"Sold a beautiful diamond watch today," Mom replied with a huge smile. "Tourist buying an anniversary present for his wife."

"That's great," Ren said as they finished with the groceries. While her mom climbed the ladder up to the boat deck, Ren picked up all the bags and carted them into the kitchen.

The kitchen was Ren's second favorite place on the houseboat after her room. The sink, stove, and refrigerator were all on the wall to the left, while the counter for food prep and a small table took up most of the right side, along with cabinets and a pantry.

Ren sat down at the table, primarily to stay out of her mother's way as she started chopping up vegetables for that night's dinner. If her mom needed help, she'd let Ren know.

Mom chatted easily about her day, the customers she'd served, the jewelry she'd sold. Ren didn't take offense that her mom hadn't asked her about her own day. Her parents weren't comfortable with the fact that Ren regularly performed magic as part of her job, particularly as they were so mundane they couldn't see it.

Ren didn't mean to yawn midway through her mother's story, but she just couldn't help it. "Sorry," she said when her mom shot her a look. "Long day."

"There might be an opening at the warehouse," Mom said hesitatingly. She didn't look at Ren but kept her face down. "I could put in a word for you there."

Ren kept her sigh to herself. "Thanks, Mom, but I prefer being a messenger." A warehouse job would be just as bad as a factory job, at least as far as Ren was concerned. She'd have to get up at the same time every day, do the exact same thing all the time. Plus, the pay wouldn't be anywhere nearly as good as what she made as a messenger.

To say nothing of how she'd react to all the electronics, the lights, the noise.

While her parents mostly understood that Ren was different, they sometimes still seemed to have the opinion that if she just tried harder, she'd fit in better. Like her birthmark—maybe she could just cover up her differences.

"It's such a dangerous job, though," Mom said. "Dealing with aliens and always being on the water."

Ren was never sure what Mom meant by that. The job had a high mortality rate, sure. But that was those other messengers, the ones who went through portals. Ren was on the water all the time. It wasn't as if there were terrible creatures just waiting to snatch her off her raft, or even bad storms. She would be more miserable when the rainy season came, but everyone was at that time. Baohu Bay was sheltered enough that it didn't get typhoons, and when a storm did blow up, there were generally enough weather satellites to drain off the winds before they came close to shore.

Unless the satellites failed. As the pumps seemed to have on Market Canal.

"Say, Mom, have you heard anything about the pumps and the canals?" Ren asked. As her parents could use personal electronics, they stayed much more on top of the news than she did.

"Not that I can recall," Mom said after pausing a moment, thinking. "Why?"

Ren told her about the dead water in the canal, how awful it had seemed to her.

Mom looked at Ren with her lips pressed together tightly.

"What?" Ren said. Obviously, her mother wanted to say something.

"Are you sure that there was a problem with the water itself? Not that you were being overly sensitive to it?" Mom asked.

Ren opened her mouth then shut it again. She knew that the canal water wasn't as fresh as the bay water. She'd noticed that before. But surely it wasn't just her sensitivities, was it?

"I don't think it was just me," Ren said, regretting having said anything. Maybe her mom was right, though. Maybe it was just her. She'd have to go back and look at the canal again, later.

Because surely someone else would have noticed if the water was starting to spoil. Right?

# FIVE

Ren spent all of the next day out on the water, ferrying passengers between the islands as well as to the mainland. She told herself that it was enough, that the power she had to push her raft across the water was more than ample. She didn't need to become a wizard. She really didn't want to become some sort of warehouse or factory worker. The water calmed her, as did being outside all day, away from all the electronics of the modern world.

When Ren checked her schedule for the following day, she saw that her first stop was at one of the *Huli* offices. She assumed that she had a delicate package to pick up there, to be delivered to someone on one of the islands. As *Huli* Transport had several offices downtown, she wasn't surprised that she'd never been to this particular building before.

At least this office was off the southern-most canal and not Market Canal. The four canals were named South, Main, Market, and North. Ren took a water taxi almost up to the door of the building, the jetty being close so Important People didn't have far to walk.

The building turned out to be one of the newer buildings in New Hong Kong, all glass and steel, thirty floors tall. The glass had been tinted a light blue and reflected the clouds, like a second sky. The lobby was wide open and three stories high, with sunlight streaming through the glass. Despite the large number of businesspeople having important conversations, sounds were muted there.

Ren walked over to the reception area. A very calm looking woman stood behind the semi-circular desk, looking regal as she fielded every query. "How may I help you?" she said when it was Ren's turn, sounding sincere, as if Ren's inquiry was as important as everyone else's.

Ren read the package number off her pager. She expected it to be one of the boxes piled up on the credenza behind the reception desk. Instead, the reception woman directed her to one of the express elevators that went straight up to the top executive floors.

Maybe the package needed to be signed for. Ren had had to do that before. It generally involved not only signing her name, but using a drop of her own blood, then mashing her thumb in it, as a print.

She enjoyed the fast, quiet speed of the elevator. The back of it was glass, and she got to look out as she flew up above the city. While Ren preferred to have her feet on the ground, or in the water, she didn't have an aversion to heights.

The lobby she stepped into was nearly silent. Any conversations being held were done in whispers. The carpet was the best quality, she was certain, with a pretty green and gold pattern that looked expensive, not like a cheap hotel. Real wood made up the wall behind the reception desk— possibly imported from Earth. It had that grainy look. The reception area reminded Ren of the main gate for a fortress. No matter how polite the male secretary sitting behind the wide expanse of a desk, he was surely a formidable dragon if you were trying to get by him and didn't have your business properly sorted out.

At least the secretary behind the desk smiled at Ren as she came up. His suit was just as nice as most of the businesspeople's she'd seen in the building. "Mr. Wang will see you right away," he said, directing her toward the door on his right, just behind his domain.

Ren stiffened. Surely not the same Mr. Wang that she'd met two days before?

She took a deep breath, calming herself. The quiet of the office suddenly felt like a trap, the world around her holding its breath. Then she marched through the door the secretary had indicated.

It turned out to lead to a conference room. The same manager she'd met before—Mr. Wang—stood at the head of a table that took up most of the space. Floor to ceiling windows covered one of the walls. The rest of the room looked utilitarian, not opulent—where workers met the managers, before being judged worthy of being invited to the fancier parts of the floor.

"Ah, Miss Ren. Please, come in," Mr. Wang said most graciously.

Today, he wore a dark colored suit jacket with a red power tie. Ren could tell that magic had been woven into the fabric of it. Normally, wizards used a piece of jewelry as a battery, for storing extra power they could easily tap into. Metal was easy to enchant and it held a charge for longer.

This man's very clothes could be used to store magical energy.

He must be very important indeed, to be able to afford such things.

The door closed automatically behind Ren, making it feel even more like a trap.

"How can I help, sir?" Ren said, falling back into the

mode of a polite messenger. She stood at the opposite end of the conference table, feet a comfortable distance apart, her hands behind her back. "What would you like for me to deliver today?"

Mr. Wang nodded, as if agreeing to play her game.

But the smile he gave her promised that he was intent on winning.

"I have a delicate magical vase that needs the utmost care," he said. "You'll have to be very careful delivering it."

Ren waited for him to continue, or at the very least, to tell her where she could go pick up the package.

"The location is a bit different," he said slowly. "You'll be going to a river world."

Ren felt her eyes grow big. She was going to have to travel by portal? That didn't bode well. However, she didn't say anything. He'd asked which wizard she normally worked with. He knew that she normally didn't work with portals.

"Li Ho is waiting for you in the transfer room," Mr. Wang said. "I expect you to be prompt and to return to me with your reply."

Mr. Wang appeared to be waiting for her to say something, so Ren replied, "I will."

"The secretary will give you directions," Mr. Wang said. "I will see you later."

Ren turned and walked out of the conference room, confused.

Surely Mr. Wang had other messengers that he could use for this? Or had he been looking for someone who would be good on the water? And what exactly was a river world?

All things that she'd find out soon enough, whether she wanted to or not.

THE TRANSFER ROOM turned out to be in one of the underground floors of the building. Li Ho was a tiny, ancient wizard who looked at her strangely when she entered. He wore a light green suit that looked as expensive as Mr. Wang's, though just the bright red jewel in his tie clip was magical. Li Ho's hair was silver and lines of age and wisdom crossed his forehead. He had a very large nose, as if his ancestors had mingled with Anglos at some point. His hands were like claws, all the fat from his body worn away and settled into the paunch at his waist.

The room was dimly lit with no windows. Ren knew that it was magically closed off from the rest of the world. If a hitchhiker came through the portal, the demon wouldn't be able to go on a killing rampage. The walls were painted the traditional dark blue-gray, the original color of the paint that prevented magic from seeping through.

What surprised Ren was that not one, but two portals had been conjured. They stood eight feet tall and at least five feet wide. Gray smoke rolled around the edges of them, crackling with blue lightning. The centers of each were a black miasma, breathing out coldness.

A small creek had been conjured to flow across the floor between the two portals. A raft, very similar to the one she normally used, was staked in the middle of it, tied to ropes anchored at both sides.

Li Ho handed Ren a small mechanical watch. "Electronic time-keepers won't work where you're going," he said gruffly.

Ren remembered that from her training: most electronics wouldn't work in a pocket world that had been carved out of regular space. It took powerful magic to create such a place, as well as more than one wizard working in concert. Electronics tended to fizzle out completely in such a place. Ren had heard horror stories from other messengers about forgotten phones or other electronics exploding upon arrival.

"How long do I have?" Ren asked as she attached the watch to the lanyard that held her ident card.

Li Ho nodded at her as if he approved of her actions. "Three hours," he said. "If you don't return by then, we'll assume you're dead."

Ren found herself swallowing against a dry throat. Other messengers faced this every day. She'd just been lucky so far that she hadn't had to.

What did Mr. Wang have against her, to be sending her into such a dangerous situation?

"What am I delivering? And to whom?" Ren asked as the wizard didn't add anything more.

"The vase is already strapped to your raft," Li Ho replied.

Only now did Ren notice the small wooden crate that was tied to the center of the raft. What looked like a regular paddle lay on the floor beside the small creek that merrily burbled between the two portals.

"Who is the package going to?" Ren asked. It wouldn't do to just go to this river world and never deliver her package.

All messengers took solemn vows: to deliver their message or to die trying. Ren had never faced that second part before.

Li Ho gave her a wintery smile. "The person at the end of the river," he said.

When Ren realized that the wizard wasn't going to give her more information, she gave him a sharp nod and walked over to the creek. She picked up her paddle and stepped onto the raft, automatically centering herself.

Though she hadn't noticed it before, the creek had a strong current running through it. Once the raft was untied, it would shoot forward.

Ren readied herself, placing herself carefully at the rear of the craft on the tongue sticking out the back, paddle in hand. She nodded at the wizard.

With a wave of his hand, Li Ho untied the raft. It immediately raced down the creek, heading toward the portal.

Ren prepared herself to enter the dark swirling mass.

Did Li Ho wish her luck, right at the end?

She suspected she was going to need it, wherever it was that she was going.

---

THE BLACKNESS of the heart of the portal didn't last for long. Ren found the coldness lingered, making her shiver.

As soon as she popped out the other side, Ren shoved her paddle down into the water, seeing if she could touch bottom. There, to the side. The current wasn't that strong, so the raft wasn't shooting out from under her feet.

Then she deliberately looked around. She'd need to come back to this exact spot to re-enter the portal and get back to Jung Wa. So she needed to see the location before she continued down river.

Or portals. There were two, in fact, tall and dark, cackling with energy. It appeared that Li Ho had taken a portion of the river from here and set it back on Jung Wa. There was still some water remaining in the river in between the two portals, so she'd be able to float the raft back through.

Li Ho must be a very strong wizard to be able to maintain not just one, but two portals at the same time.

The river here was only ten feet wide and not very deep. The sky was the wrong shade of blue, dark with too much purple mixed in, despite the sun shining down from almost directly above her head. The air smelled of the river and fresh water, marshes still blooming and not yet gone to seed.

Just a few feet from where Ren stood, a second river flowed. She couldn't tell for certain, but she'd bet that the current of the other river went in the direction opposite to the river she floated on.

In the distance, on either side, more rivers flowed. Only a few traveled in straight lines. The rest appeared to crisscross each other over the plain and up the small hills on either side. It was just river after river, some running so close there was barely a foot of land between them.

Though Ren couldn't say for certain, she had the feeling that the valley she floated in was the only place that existed in this entire world: that a formless abyss swirled just beyond the hills on either side.

Why would a wizard create a world that was full of rivers? It didn't make any sense. Unless they were trying to practice a particular type of water magic? Did wizards do that?

As Ren wasn't very powerful, she only knew the basics of magic. Most magic was transformational, scaling up or down, turning a drop of water into a lake, a single stone into a wall, or a tree into a toothpick. Her own magical practice generally involved taking the existing currents of the water and making them flow for her, propelling her raft forward. It was part of the reason why she didn't really like the canal taxies—they worked against the regular patterns of the water.

Ren looked downriver, trying to see what was ahead of her. Where was the end of the river? Who would be at the end?

She pulled out the time piece. According to it, it was currently nine AM.

She had until noon to deliver her package and return, else she'd be stuck here for good.

Ren lifted her paddle and let the river carry her away, adding a touch of her own magic to increase her speed.

She didn't have that long to deliver her package. And she'd just as soon be home for dinner.

# SIX

It took Ren about fifty minutes for her to reach her destination. She didn't understand why wizards couldn't more accurately place messengers where they needed to go. She'd certainly heard the other messengers bitch about it constantly. She'd always felt sorry for them, as she'd never had to work with wizards on a regular basis.

At least the river helped her along, the current pushing her in the right direction.

The sameness of the landscape bothered her. She was used to wide water with different islands coming into view. This was just constant grassy banks with nothing to look at, for what she assumed were miles. Plus, there were no birds, no fish, no insects or butterflies. It was a world dedicated to rivers and that was it. No real wind either. All she heard was the quiet sound of water talking to itself.

Finally, a gray shape rose up on the right bank. It resolved into a one-story wooden building.

As Ren drew closer, the river shrank abruptly. It went from being ten feet wide to five. She could now see the stones of the river bottom clearly as the water grew more shallow. The grass died out as well, and the area turned into a rocky plain. The hills in the distance were now covered in a gray fog, as if the morning mist had yet to dissipate.

Ren stayed on her raft until she ran out of water and the raft started scraping the river bottom, unable to go any further downstream. She was still at least seventy feet from the building. She dragged her raft up onto the riverbank, though she doubted that it would float away if she didn't.

The package had been tied to the raft with long rubber straps that instantly snapped back into a much smaller size when she unhooked them. Though they'd originally been stretched out over four feet, hooking into the edges of her raft, they shrank down to about six inches.

Handy. She'd never seen fasteners like that before. They were branded with the little *Huli* Transport fox on the ends of them. She stuck them into a pocket of her jumpsuit.

The package was a plain box, wrapped in thick brown paper, maybe eight inches on a side. It was very light. No name had been written on it. Ren had to assume that she just needed to deliver it to whoever inhabited the building in front of her.

The building itself looked like something out of a historic vid from the American old west. The wooden boards making up the building hadn't been painted gray. Instead, the wood had faded and aged and was now the same color as driftwood. A set of double doors hung in the middle of the front, solid wood and painted black, looking almost as dark as a portal. Crooked windows had been cut out on either side of the doors, filled with silvered glass, making the building seem blind. The roof was flat, which told Ren that despite the rivers, there was no rain here.

No grass grew next to the building. In fact, there was no greenery anywhere close. It was as if the gray of the building wouldn't allow any competing color, preferring to stand apart, aloof. The silence was oppressive. Ren walked carefully, wincing at the way her shoes crunched against the gravel. The air smelled of baked dirt and dust.

Ren paused when she reached the doors. There was no obvious bell or door knocker. She rapped on one of the doors with her knuckles. The door swung open a little, obviously unlocked.

"Hello? Anyone here?" Ren called out.

"Come on in," came the faint reply from inside.

Ren took a deep breath to steady herself. She was just delivering a package to a mysterious client. That was it. There were tremendous penalties for putting messengers into harm's way by signing a bad contract with a client.

She pushed her way into the building, pausing for a moment to let her eyes adjust to the dimness inside. The room continued the theme from the outside, looking like a saloon from the American west. A bar took up the entire left wall, though only three bottles were stocked on the wide shelves behind it. The mirror behind the bar didn't reflect anything but darkness. Thick wooden beams painted black crossed the high ceiling, and tough, scarred wood made up the floor. Large round tables filled the area, with a dozen cheap wooden chairs scattered around each.

A single occupant sat toward the back. Cards were laid out on the table in front of him, suits and colors Ren didn't recognize.

She walked directly over to the man, saying, "I have a package for you."

He didn't look up, but continued to study the cards before him. "From whom?"

His voice sounded familiar, though Ren couldn't place it. "Wang Guanki," she said, proud of how her own voice sounded so strong, despite the strange situation.

The man looked up, obviously surprised.

"So what does my brother want?" he asked. Then he paused and gave a low long whistle. "Or was it the messenger that he wanted me to see?"

Ren was too shocked to reply. The man seated in front of her looked exactly like Mr. Wang. The color of their suits was different though both were made of the same high quality, with strong magic woven into the cloth. But that was the only difference. They had the same black hair, the same knowing smile, the same cruel-looking eyes.

"This—this is the package, sir," Ren managed to stammer out, shoving the box in his direction.

"Put it on the table, there," the man said. He leaned back and looked at her. "So you're a messenger for my brother's company. *Huli* Transport. That benevolent dictatorship that he supports."

"I am," Ren said after she put the package on the table. She wasn't sure about *Huli* being a dictatorship, though. "Do you have any reply for Mr. Wang?"

"What do you know of the history of *Huli* Transport?" the man asked instead. "In particular, the creation of the portal beacons?"

"Just what we're taught in school, sir," Ren said, managing to still sound normal despite how much she wanted to just run away.

The man made a circling motion with his hand, indicating that Ren should continue.

"The beacons were created by an insane scientist, back on Earth," Ren said. "He was the first to discover the area where physics and magic met, and started the process to map out where the two crossed."

"And what of his partner?"

"Who?" Ren asked. Had she learned anything about the man's partner?

"Ao Dan? The warlock?"

Ren frowned. She didn't remember anything about a warlock, particularly one being associated with the creation of the portals. *Huli* Transport employed wizards, those whose magic followed law. She'd never met a warlock, the ones who used chaotic magic.

"Ao Dan is a powerful warlock," the man said. "He was as responsible for the portal beacons as anyone else. He was the one who pushed the development of all portals along, giving mankind the stars."

Ren didn't know what to say. She'd never heard of Ao Dan, or any warlock for that matter, who had been vital to anything.

"Have you ever met a warlock? Worked with one?" the man asked.

"I have not," Ren replied. The company didn't employ them. There was something wrong with their magic. They were unstable.

"Well, you have now," the man said. "I am Wang Dali, and I am a warlock."

"I see," Ren said. Was it against company policy to deliver to warlocks? Probably not. One of the tenets of the magical arm of *Huli* Transport was that it was strictly neutral in all deliveries, and would serve anyone who paid, as long as they didn't put their messengers in harms' way.

When Dali didn't continue, Ren asked, "Do you have a message for your brother? The other Mr. Wang?"

Dali continued to stare at Ren. "Why do you wear your hair like that?" he said. "I don't mean to give offense. But Ao Dan wears his hair in a similar fashion."

A warlock? Did they think she was a warlock? Or associated with this Ao Dan? She'd never even heard of him before!

With a shaking hand, Ren drew back the curtain of hair

hanging over her right cheek. "To hide this, sir," she said quietly.

"A mark that cannot be removed. Interesting," Dali said after a moment. He nodded to himself. "Tell my brother that I am not interested."

Ren didn't know what that meant. Was he not interested in her? In something else? In the package? She had no idea, and hoped that she never would have to learn.

While the original Mr. Wang, back on Jung Wa, was a very powerful magician, she had no doubt that his brother Dali was considerably stronger.

"Here." Dali picked a card off the table, then threw it at her. As it spun through the air, Ren would swear that she saw the face of it change. The back remained the same—a stylized river motif in black and white that appeared the exact same no matter which direction the card faced.

The front turned into a card she was more familiar with —the rain man card from a flower card deck. A blue river flowed behind the figure who held an umbrella, with a leaping frog at his feet. However, instead of showing Ono no Michikaze, the figure looked like a Seidaren, with blue-green skin and yellow fuzz covering its head, wearing what looked suspiciously like her own brown jumpsuit. The figure's face was turned partially away, so just a single eye could be seen.

Ren wasn't sure why the one eye bothered her so much, given her own predilections, but it did.

"Consider that your tip," Dali said. "Oh, and also tell my brother that this place is now closed, as the cards have foretold. I will be moving the game somewhere else. You better leave now. And hurry."

Ren didn't have to be told twice. She wasn't sure exactly what it entailed, but she assumed that Dali was about to destroy this river world.

She didn't want to think about what would happen if she was trapped in here when it disappeared.

Ren bowed her head and hurried out of the building, racing toward her raft. As she reached it, she heard a rushing sound from behind her.

Gray clouds gathered across the horizon. The sound grew louder, as if a waterfall was approaching.

Ren dragged her raft up the river she'd come down, getting to a spot where the water was deeper. However, the current fought her now. It wanted her to stay there, at the end of the river. She pushed hard with her magic, as well as paddled, making her way slowly upriver, but it wasn't going to be fast enough.

Not with those gray clouds approaching. The sound of a waterfall grew louder. Was the world going to be washed away?

Of course, Dali wouldn't have thought to give her a lift somewhere. No, he probably thought she was a powerful wizard. Or a warlock. Whatever. Not just a mere messenger.

Ren glanced over to her left. There was another river right there, just a few feet away, across the grass that was rapidly turning yellow. It appeared to have a current that went in the right direction. Did she risk it?

Staying on her current course wasn't likely to get her out in time.

Ren drove her raft to the riverbank, then stepped out onto the earth, immediately sinking knee deep into freezing cold water. Damn it! The rivers weren't separated by solid land so much as swamp. At least the water was clean and didn't reek. She expended even more magic, floating the raft over to the next river, quickly scrambling back up on top of it.

Despite the warm sunlight shining down on her, she

found herself shivering. That water was freezing, as if it carried the cold of the abyss.

At least the current on this river urged her along in the right direction. However, she still faced a gray mass of clouds.

Ren tried to focus. She paddled as fast as she could, keeping up a steady stream of magic to push her raft along.

It was so hard to focus! The sound of rushing water grew louder, becoming a physical force—not quite as bad as being surrounded by machines running electricity, but almost. The grass on either riverbank withered before her eyes, getting sucked under the water. Clouds now filled the sky, threatening rain, though she still didn't feel any wind. Her shoulders and arms ached with the constant motion, but she dared not stop.

There! The portals finally showed up in the distance.

Of course, they were on the other river.

Ren pushed her way along. Could she use her magic to float her raft across? Between the two rivers?

Now, the current of the river she was on grew stronger. The roar of the water grew even more deafening, as if it could flatten her with sound alone.

Ren fought against the river, needing to stop herself before she shot past the portals across the way. She poured out more magic while angling the raft toward the bank. She kept her feet firmly on the craft as she struggled to get it to turn. The paddle slipped in her hands, the river trying to steal it away from her. The muscles across her back strained as she slowly pushed the front of the raft around, heading toward the bank. Her magic crackled around her as she struggled to control the raft on the runaway current.

There was nothing solid for Ren to land the front of the raft against. She rammed forward, against the murky, matted grass that masked the stagnant, freezing water underneath.

Could she lift the raft up and float across to the other

river? There was nothing to push against. The river she was on kept wanting to flip the rear of the raft around.

The clear image of Dali flipping that card came back to her. It spiraled lazily through the air, floating to her hand.

She couldn't push her way straight across the watery mess, but maybe she could spin her way there.

Ren changed sides on the raft and let the back of it come forward and around. She performed a slow spiral across the grassy remains that separated the two rivers until she nosed against the river with the portals on it.

It wasn't until Ren was facing the other way that she realized exactly what was happening to the world, how Dali was destroying it. The end of the river now reached the top of the sky and possibly beyond, curling slightly forward. Water poured down, forming the massive gray clouds she saw. It was as if the river was being rolled up on itself.

Ren pushed herself forward, driving herself toward the far portal of Li Ho. She paddled herself through the gray oval, the biting cold freezing her wet skin.

The raft came to a rough halt as she left the water and encountered the concrete floor of the transfer room. Ren stumbled but maintained her balance and stayed standing on the raft.

Li Ho gave her an appraising eye. "You made it," he said.

Ren nodded. Her arms shook from all the effort she'd put into escaping. Her legs felt funny, as if she were no longer used to being on solid ground. She silently handed the old wizard the mechanical time piece, noting that at least according to it, she had over an hour to spare.

A dry screech from behind Ren made her jump. The water flowing between the two portals abruptly dried up. She heard the faint roar of the waterfalls echoing in the space. A strange wind filled the transfer room.

"Dali is destroying the river world," Ren told Li Ho.

"You should have said something sooner," Li Ho scolded her, collapsing the portals before something else could come through, or possibly this world be sucked into that one as it disappeared.

"Sorry," Ren said. She hadn't known. She didn't work with wizards and portals.

Hopefully, this would be the last time in a long, long while.

# SEVEN

Ren's day was far from over. She was still soaking wet from the knees down, but she couldn't go and change her clothes. She needed to deliver Dali's message to Guanki, then check her schedule. She believed that she had to go pick up a passenger from the island of Ra Po and ferry them to the mainland. Plus whatever else had been added to her day by dispatch.

The elevator from the basement disgorged her on the main floor, where she had to make her way over to reception to announce that she had a message to deliver to Mr. Wang.

Ren shifted uncomfortably at the rear of the elevator. The disapproval from the other passengers was palpable. She didn't think it was just because she was a messenger. No, though she couldn't smell it, there was a chance that she smelled like the swamp water she was still soaked with.

If only she had stronger magic! No, that wasn't it. She might have had enough power. She did not have enough control. She could have dried her clothes if she'd been outside in a clear space and if she weren't so exhausted. In the crowded lobby or elevator, she couldn't risk it. She might damage the people surrounding her, overheat herself or her clothes. And it wouldn't do to just appear before Mr. Wang not wearing anything at all.

So Ren put up with the stares and not-so-quiet whispers about her by the other passengers on the elevator. She was used to the quiet speculation about her hair after all, what she was hiding behind it.

The male secretary on the executive floor managed to both smile at her as well as wrinkle his nose at the same time. He ushered her into the same conference room she'd been in before, letting her know that Mr. Wang would be joining her shortly.

Ren walked over to the window and looked down on New Hong Kong. She was facing northwest. The city itself was roughly shaped like a fan, with the bay across the bottom scalloped edge, the four waterways like wavy spines. The city narrowed down to a single point to the west, where the Munda River ended, its powerful waters tamed and split into the canals.

From here, Market Canal looked like the other waterways, just a dark gray snake of water winding its way between the buildings. Was it dying? If she had time, she might go to the start of it to check, to see if there was just something wrong with her or with the water itself.

When the door opened, Ren turned around to face Mr. Wang. She peered at him curiously, trying to discern the differences between him and his brother.

Dali was thinner, his cheekbones more prominent. But the physical differences were minimal.

Ren realized that it was primarily a feeling that separated the brothers. Mr. Wang felt more stiff, more formal, more like an artificial lake at a monastery, while Dali was more like his rivers, wild and uncontrollable.

"You have a message for me?" Mr. Wang asked formally.

"I do, sir," Ren said. She widened her stance and put her hands behind her back. Like all messengers, she'd been trained to not only remember the exact words of a client, but to repeat with some accuracy the tone and intonation of the words.

"He had two things to say. The first, 'Tell my brother that I am not interested.'"

Mr. Wang seemed surprised at that. "Really?" he said.

"The second thing Wang Dali said was, 'Oh, and also tell my brother that this place is now closed, as the cards have foretold. I will be moving the game somewhere else.'"

That didn't surprise Mr. Wang at all. "Very good," he said. "Did you see his cards?"

"They were laid out on the table in front of him," Ren said. Should she tell him about the card he'd given her? She fished it out from her front pocket. "He gave me this card. Told me it was a tip."

She held out the card to Mr. Wang. He came closer to her and studied it carefully with his own hands behind his back, as if he dared not touch the card himself.

"Interesting," he said. He pressed his lips together before he said, "I don't mean to give offense, but would you like some help drying your outfit?"

Ren didn't blush, that wasn't in her nature. Acute embarrassment still made her cheeks grow slightly warm. Humiliation ate at her core, making her want to fold in on herself, collapsing like a wet origami flower.

"If it wouldn't be too much bother," Ren said, keeping her voice down but her words strong, refusing to mumble.

A refreshing wind blew around her. She suddenly realized the stench she'd been carrying was gone. Her skin no longer itched. In fact, some of her energy was suddenly back as well.

"Thank you," Ren said. Why couldn't she do something simple like that for herself?

She handed Mr. Wang the card.

"Oh no. That's yours. You should keep it," he said. "It might bring you luck."

Ren shrugged and slipped it back into her pocket. She wasn't sure what the card might bring her, but she suspected just throwing it away would bring offense.

"Anything else, sir?" Ren asked.

"No, that's all. Thank you for your service," Mr. Wang said more formally, bowing his head to her.

He stayed where he was as she let herself out of the conference room. It wasn't until she left the building that she started to feel like herself again, as if she'd rejoined the rest of the world and she could finally breathe.

---

FORTUNATELY, it turned out that Ren had several hours before she had another passenger to pick up. When she checked her account, she saw that she'd received a hazard pay bonus for her work that morning.

Evidently, having to flee a world before it was destroyed counted as being more dangerous than usual for a messenger. That was good to know.

Normally, Ren would leave New Hong Kong as soon as she was able to, maybe spend the time before her next passenger out on one of the smaller, calmer islands. However, this afternoon, as she had a few hours to kill before she had to fetch her raft and go out to Ra Po, she decided to check on Market Canal.

She looked carefully at South Canal before she boarded a water taxi back down to the bay. The water in this canal was slightly stale, as she'd expected. It wasn't dead, though.

Once she'd reached the bay, Ren took a ferry across, traveling from South Canal to Market Canal. The pier she got off on was a transfer point between the bay and the canal. However, Ren didn't immediately take a taxi up the canal. Instead, she walked up the side of the water.

At the base, where the canal met the bay, the water was fresher. Within two blocks, it grew stale and dank. Within another block, it had had grown even worse.

Ren couldn't say why she felt that the water was now dead, just that it was. No fish lived there anymore. Nor any healthy organism. It was just…dead.

It wasn't her imagination. There was something wrong with the canal. But what? And who could she tell?

---

REN PAUSED as she passed by a hair salon. They promised the latest styles, which appeared to be hair longer than hers on the right side and braided into some sort of fashionable pattern.

Should she get her hair cut? But that would mean showing her birthmark to the world. She didn't want to do that. She could maybe start to wear some sort of cover on her cheek, hide it that way. She would have to get that first, before she got her haircut.

However, then she'd have to remember to apply it every morning. And then reapply it when it got wet, or if she sweat it off during the day, being on the water under the hot sun. She had a hat that she wore to keep the sun off her face, but it wouldn't be enough.

If only there were a way to permanently remove her birthmark! Maybe she should go back to the doctor's office, let them do a skin graft. It would be painful. She'd have to take some time off work. And she wasn't certain it would work, that her birthmark wouldn't grow into the new skin.

If Ren was completely honest with herself, while she hated the mark that made her look so different than everyone else, she also wore it with some pride. It did mark her as different. She wasn't the same as everyone else, the factory workers or the clerks. Her job was different. Her life was different. She was different.

In the end, Ren decided to not change her hair. Anyone who knew her knew that she was a good girl. She followed the law, and did the right thing. Anyone who thought she was a chaotic warlock just had to get to know her.

---

REN WAS SURPRISED to learn that night that the city government published daily statistics on the waterways, including pH and water levels. Dad showed her the site on their home terminal after they'd finished eating dinner.

"See?" he said, pointing at the screen. They were in the living room that had once been her brothers' room. A large, flat screen covered one wall that the family used either for watching vids or for accessing the local network. The family had only bought it once the boys had moved out. Before then, everyone just used their personal comm, while Ren had used public terminals.

Ren saw the numbers in black and white. Everything looked normal according to the machines that monitored the waterway. That couldn't be right. Her shoulders were still tense and her stomach was still knotted from looking at the water that afternoon. She'd barely been able to eat dinner.

"Can you bring up a week's worth of numbers?" Ren asked, not believing what she was seeing. There had to be something wrong with the monitoring equipment.

Dad obliged, showing a range of data.

Ren focused on the water levels. The numbers were the same, day after day. That didn't make any sense. There were tides, right? Shouldn't the numbers be going up and down?

"Can you look at the numbers for another canal?" Ren said. "Like, South Canal?" She knew that one was healthy.

"Sure thing," Dad said, flashing her an indulgent smile. He didn't understand her any better than her mom did, but he was always kind about it.

He'd taken off his nice office shirt and tie, and wore a sleeveless white undershirt with his good dress pants, with bare feet and house slippers. The temperature on the water was cooler than in the city, but it was still warm. The houseboat had air conditioning; however, Ren's mom and dad didn't like turning it on unless it was midsummer and the temperature was stupidly hot.

Her dad looked both young and old at the same time. Ren remembered when her dad's hair had been all black, with no fine white hairs glinting along the sides. His chest was still wide and his arms still had muscles from hauling nets on the weekends, when the family sailed into the bay and went fishing. She remembered thinking he was the strongest man in the world for the longest time. However, his skin was no longer as firm as it once had been. The dark brown color of his eyes was fading. And sometimes he had an old man smell now, more like her grandparents, sour and pungent.

Ren didn't know what she'd do once her parents actually grew old. She couldn't even consider what would happen after they died.

Her dad pulled up South Canal numbers. There was only a small change in the water levels, nothing significant, but it was present.

"See?" Ren said, pointing out the difference. "The

amount of water in the canal should change. Not a lot, but every day it should shift up and down a little."

"Huh," Dad said. He split the screen so they could look at the numbers side by side.

Ren was right. The numbers showing the water level stayed exactly the same day after day on Market Canal, but not on South Canal.

Dad pulled up the numbers on all four canals at the same time. The other three changed regularly, as Ren had expected them to. Only Market Canal didn't.

"There's something wrong with the monitoring equipment," Dad said, frowning. "It's not reporting correctly."

"So you believe me?" Ren said, relieved. She hadn't realized just how much more tense she'd gotten since dinner.

"Of course we do!" Dad said. He turned in his chair to face her. "We've always believed you. We knew that there was something…special with you, early on, you know. Particularly given how you'd cry every time we took you off the water." He gave her a huge smile. "You're our special, beautiful girl, Meiren."

Ren smiled and nodded, squeezing her dad's proffered hand. Her parents weren't perfect. They had done their best with her, such an unusual child.

No matter what her dad said, though, they hadn't always believed her, didn't always believe her, even now. It was good that there were some numbers finally, to back up what she knew to be true about Market Canal.

Dad sent a message off to the people in charge of the monitoring equipment, letting them know that there was a problem with it.

Ren finally went to bed, exhausted from the long day and adventures. She'd done what she could about the canal, pointing out the problem to the officials. Surely the water council would look into it, and fix the canal.

She dreamed of rivers flowing all around her, crisscrossing in front and behind her. She had to choose one, she knew. But which one? None of the water rushing by appealed to her. She stayed frozen in fear of making the wrong choice as the world moved on around her.

# EIGHT

REN WAS happy to hear that her dad received a message back from the water council, assuring him that they'd look into the monitoring equipment, thanking him for bringing the issue to their attention.

She could finally get back to doing her job, leading her normal life. She had regular passengers and packages that day, ferrying people and things across the bay to the islands and back.

Ren wasn't sure why she felt the need to verify the numbers of the canal again that night. She stopped at one of the public terminals and called up the monitoring site again.

The amount of water in Market Canal now reflected the actual ebb and flow of the tides. That was good.

However, Ren had seen those numbers before.

She pulled up the numbers on South Canal again.

The numbers didn't match. Not exactly. They were off by exactly point eight.

Whoever had "fixed" Market Canal had done it by tying the numbers of the two canals together, then off-setting them just enough that a first look wouldn't immediately show that there was a problem.

Ren would bet that if she looked long enough, she'd see a relationship between all the other stats reported on Market Canal and the other waterways, that all the numbers were being generated, that nothing being reported was real.

Why? Who was intent on killing Market Canal? What was their objective? It made no sense to Ren. Were they just intent on violating the treaty with the Seidaren?

Now, no one would believe her when she pointed out that there was a problem. And the people who were in charge were aware that someone was looking, and would be more on guard.

Who could Ren tell? How could she get people to look at Market Canal and fix it, before it was too late?

---

REN WAS CONSIDERING CALLING it an early day the next day when her pager vibrated. With a sigh, she docked her raft at the small pier of the closest island and went looking for a terminal. She found a plain screen attached to a pole at the end of the pier. A retractable black hood covered it.

Though Ren hated being so boxed in, she still stepped in close to the terminal and pulled the hood down over her head so that she could see and hear in private. The sour smell of baked plastic made her wrinkle her nose. The air grew still and hard to breathe.

Ren hurriedly punched in the number for dispatch, calling up her account. A special request had been placed, with the passenger specifically requesting her to ferry them from the mainland to one of the islands.

The world tilted when she saw that Hanshu wanted her to ferry him home, back to Hudie Dao, the Butterfly Island.

All of the upheaval in her life had been caused by him. Did she really want to see him again?

But he was a regular. And she couldn't afford to say no to a client.

The sun was low in the sky over New Hong Kong when Ren arrived at the main pier just off South Canal. Hanshu stood there, waving at her as always, as if he was excited to see her.

She suspected he was just happy to finally be leaving the city again. Or maybe he had to wave that way to make sure that she'd notice him, as most of the rest of the people on the pier appeared to be ignoring him or didn't realize he was standing there until he moved.

Instead of being dressed like a factory worker, Hanshu wore an incredibly expensive suit. It was as if he and the Wang brothers all went to the same tailor. Hanshu's suit was the color of soft gray fog that melted away when the sun came out, with a pale blue shirt and a dark, rich purple tie. He looked elegant in ways that normal people didn't—as if he'd been selected to play the ideal successful businessman for a movie and filled the part perfectly.

"Good to see you! Good to see you!" Hanshu said enthusiastically as he leaped down off the pier and landed lightly on the raft while Ren held it steady.

"Good to see you too, sir," Ren said. "Would you care for a bench or a chair?"

"No, thank you," Hanshu said. He turned and faced the front of the raft, hands behind his back as Ren maneuvered the craft around and got them headed out into the bay.

It wasn't until they'd left the immediate area of the docks and were out on the water proper that Hanshu asked, "Did you get yourself tested?"

"I did," Ren said. "I have gotten stronger. As well as more sensitive." She still didn't know what would happen to her when her sensitivities grew so bad that she'd be disabled, no longer to live in the city at all.

Would she end up a hermit on one of the islands? Living in caves or on the beach? Unable to interact with anything modern or electronic?

Hanshu nodded, seeming to be satisfied. "Good. And are you happy with your position as a messenger?"

"I am, sir," Ren said. As long as she got to stay out on the water and wasn't having to deal with portals and wizards. Or warlocks, for that matter.

Hanshu looked over his shoulder at her. "Are you really?" he inquired, peering at her.

Ren shrugged. It wasn't as if she had much choice. More power didn't automatically mean more control.

Hanshu nodded as if he overheard her objections. And maybe he did. Ren still had no idea who, or really what, Hanshu actually was.

"There is something else bothering you," he said after a few moments. "What is it?"

Ren sighed. While she'd been hoping that she could bring up her concerns about Market Canal to Hanshu, she still found herself reluctant to tell him. She wasn't sure if she was more afraid that he'd tell her that it wasn't anything for her to worry about or if he said it was of great concern.

Still, she told him about Market Canal, how the water seemed dead, and how the monitoring facilities appeared to be hacked or broken.

"I am aware of the issues with Market Canal," Hanshu said slowly when she finished.

A wave of relief crashed over Ren. Someone believed her! And without her having to prove it to them! She took a deep breath, feeling even her lungs relax. Surely this powerful being would fix the situation.

"However, there isn't anything that I can do about it at this time," Hanshu continued.

Just like that, Ren felt the chill evening breezes blowing off the bay and sending shivers down her spine.

"I agree with you that something needs to be done, and soon," Hanshu said. "It's just that I only have so much time and energy to do things. And some things need more finesse than I can manage."

Ren frowned. Hanshu currently looked so elegant! How could he not possess an infinite amount of finesse as well?

"Trust me, I would do something immediately if I could," Hanshu said, trying to reassure her. He looked over his shoulder at her, squinting his eyes at the sun setting just behind her. "Do you want to try to fix it?" he asked.

Ren could tell that he was honestly curious. It was as if she were some foreign species and this was a test.

"I do," Ren said.

"Why?"

"People rely on that canal," Ren said. "Not just for transportation, but for food. There are families who fish off that river."

"True, but you don't truly care about them, do you?" Hanshu said. "It isn't as if you've ever met them." He paused, then said, "Really, why do you care? Why does it matter to you?"

Ren thought for a moment. "It isn't right," was what she finally came up with. "I know that doesn't make any sense. But it isn't right for one of our canals to be poisoned for whatever reason. It needs to be fixed. That water shouldn't be allowed to just die."

"It's the water, isn't it?" Hanshu persisted. "The dead waters bother you more than anything else. Am I right?"

"You are," Ren said. She hadn't really considered it, but that was the main thing that bothered her about the canal.

Water should never be dead, not like that. Even still water had life to it.

"All right," Hanshu said. He gave her a quick smile. "I will send someone your way who may be able to help you fix this."

"Me, sir?" Ren said, surprised. "How can I fix the canal?" It seemed so much bigger than her.

Hanshu shrugged. "You care. That should be enough."

Ren didn't think that would be anywhere near enough. There was something wrong with the monitoring equipment. Someone in the water council knew it and was covering it up.

"I can try, sir," Ren finally replied, knowing that Hanshu needed her to say something.

He beamed at her. "That's all anyone can ever ask." He grew more sober, and his eyes turned inward.

Ren blinked, surprised at the amount of power that suddenly poured off the being in front of her. She held the raft steady, afraid for a moment that it would be swamped.

Her own magical abilities were minuscule in comparison to his, like an ant facing an entire sand dune, thinking that she had to move it from one spot to the next.

But she could, one grain at a time.

"Someone should be in touch with you in the following week," Hanshu said. His voice had a strange echo to it, as if he were speaking to her from far away. "Be on the lookout for a stranger."

"I will, sir. Thank you, sir," Ren said.

Hanshu came back to himself. The power he held subsided back to its normal, shaded levels. Instead of seeming to be taller and broader, standing ten feet tall and mighty, he appeared as a dapper businessman catching a ride home on her raft.

"No, it is I who must thank you," Hanshu said. "This

business needs to be taken care of. I'm glad it's now in your hands."

Ren gulped. She knew she didn't have the magical ability, and she was certain she didn't have the *finesse* required to discover what was wrong with Market Canal, let alone fix it.

Hanshu appeared to believe in her, though. Maybe she could do it.

They rode the rest of the way to the island in silence, the darkness gathering as the sun set. Ren would still have enough light to make it back home that evening, but just barely. Fortunately, she had her own mage light she could call up to light her way.

Hanshu climbed the ladder to the pier with sure feet and hands, then disappeared quickly, swallowed by the dim evening.

Ren turned her raft around slowly, heading back home.

Who had Hanshu called? What was she supposed to do?

Hopefully, she would find out soon enough.

---

REN FOUND herself obsessed with the numbers on Market Canal. She avoided the canal itself, as the dead water always bothered her so much. However she found herself checking the public monitoring site whenever she had a few minutes between jobs.

She never checked the numbers again from her home terminal. She wondered if she'd put her family at risk by doing that. Hopefully, though, as she'd never send them another message, they'd think that she'd been lulled into complacency, that she'd believed their lies.

Instead, she checked the site from various public terminals, and never the same one twice. It would be difficult for anyone to determine a pattern as Ren's schedule stayed as erratic as always.

As far as Ren could tell, only Market Canal had issues. She'd made a point of visiting all of the waterways. While the water in the others was stale, as to be expected, it wasn't dead.

Ren also looked up warlocks on the public terminal. She was shocked to find out just how awful they were. The list of horrible things that warlocks did to society seemed endless.

Why did Mr. Wang still associate with his brother? It was his brother, on the one hand. But if he was evil…

Ren just didn't know. Both of the Wang brothers had seemed, well, not just powerful but cruel. Surely Mr. Wang was good, though.

There wasn't anything she could do about meeting a warlock. *Huli* Transport was neutral in terms of delivering to one. It bothered her more that she might be mistaken for one. She reconsidered changing her hair, but she never quite got around to it.

Ren did find herself eagerly looking at her schedule every day. Surely Hanshu would send her a passenger who would turn out to be the help he'd promised. Right?

But a week went by, and Ren didn't meet anyone new. She knew that Hanshu had done *something* when he'd been on her raft, put out some sort of call. Was the other person just ignoring Hanshu? She couldn't imagine either being so rude, or perhaps being that much stronger than Hanshu that they could safely disregard his call.

The next time Ren was called to Hudie Dao, even though the passenger didn't list their name, she assumed it was Hanshu. She paddled out on Baohu Bay early that morning. The waters seemed more still than usual, not even the occasional breeze rippling the glass-like surface. The birds were hushed as they flew over, silently cruising for the more lively land. No winds touched her skin, but she still felt trails of chicken flesh rise up across her shoulders. The sweet pork bun she'd had for breakfast no longer warmed her stomach, sitting instead like a solid lump.

As Ren passed the northern tip of the island, she saw a swath of blue butterflies weaving gracefully across the water, heading back for the trees. Just as the crops needed the butterflies to pollinate them, the city needed its canals.

Who else could she approach about the issues? She no longer trusted the water council. Even if she could somehow force them to retest the waters, they might fake the results. Could she maybe purchase her own chemistry kit and prove that the waters were wrong on her own? Would anyone believe her?

An elegant looking man stood at the end of the first pier, watching her. As he didn't wave at her, Ren knew that it was not Hanshu, though she could feel that this individual's magic was also contained. However, instead of it being hidden by a cloth shroud, it felt as though it was veiled by rainclouds.

"Good morning, sir," Ren called up as she drew close to the pier. "Do you need help onboarding?"

"I do not," came a deep familiar voice.

Where had Ren heard that voice before?

Like Hanshu, instead of climbing down the ladder from the pier to the raft, the individual leaped down, landing oh-so-lightly in the middle of her raft.

Ren stayed perfectly still, looking at the man, feeling like a small mouse in the presence of a great hawk.

The man smiled at her with his cruel mouth, his eyes sharp and hard.

"Good morning, Ren," he said after a few moments of studying her.

"Good morning, Wang Dali."

# PART TWO
# THE RULE OF MONEY

# NINE

DALI REFUSED A CHAIR OR BENCH, and instead stood like Hanshu regularly did, staring off the edge of the raft and out over the water. His suit was charcoal gray, the color of cold river water, with a bright white shirt and a ruby red tie. As before, magic had been subtly woven into the material itself. He stood stiff and proud looking over the water, as if searching for his next victim.

"It is good to see you again," Dali said after a few moments. "I'm glad you didn't change your hair."

Ren wasn't sure why that was important. "I'm not a warlock, sir," she said after a moment. Wasn't that obvious?

"I know that," Dali said. "I did some research on you. You're a messenger for *Huli* Transport, a bit stronger than expected, but you lack control. You live on a houseboat with your parents, and are sensitive to electricity."

"Yes, sir," Ren said. That did appear to sum up her life.

"You could become so much more," Dali said.

Ren pressed her lips together and refused to ask what he meant. Either he would tell her or he wouldn't. She was happy with her life as it was. Wasn't she?

"I'd like to show you. Take you up to Quiling Island, and demonstrate the potential you contain. How much stronger you could be."

A part of Ren leaped at the thought. More magic? More focus? Possibly enough control so she could live a more normal life?

But the rest of Ren felt cautious. Dali was a warlock, not a wizard. *Huli* Transport did not approve of warlocks. In fact, they frequently persecuted them. Ren could deliver Dali to where he needed to go because *Huli* Transport was officially neutral in those matters. But she shouldn't associate further with him. Right?

"It is strictly forbidden for messengers to fraternize with clients, sir." It was the best excuse she could think of to put him off.

"I could make it an official *Huli* Transport sanctioned outing," Dali said seriously. "Require you to travel far into the hills to pick up a package and deliver it."

"Why would you want to do this, sir?" Ren asked. It made no sense to her for him to be offering this opportunity. Something had to be in it for him.

Dali laughed. "You realize that I lied to my brother when I said I wasn't interested in you, right? I didn't want him to know the truth. That I could easily see you as my apprentice."

"Sir?" Ren said. She splashed her paddle into the water by accident. Cold water scattered across her calves, startling her.

"It isn't just the haircut, you know," Dali said. "You have an air about you. Something different. I suspect it's because of your sensitivities. Most warlocks have more sensitivity to electricity, though you seem to be an extreme case."

Ren blinked, surprised. Why hadn't anyone at headquarters told her that?

Then again, *Huli* Transport didn't have dealings with warlocks.

"I don't want to do evil," Ren said. There. May as well have it all out in the open.

Dali laughed harshly, the barking sound echoing out over the water. "You spent time looking up warlocks, didn't you?"

"I did, sir," Ren said.

"Don't believe everything you've read," Dali warned her. "We aren't all evil. We do good as well. We just aren't as lawful as the wizards. The company doesn't appreciate our unique take. We use a different type of magic. They consider that bad."

"You do good?" Ren asked, surprised. That hadn't been included in any of the articles she'd found on the network. "What kind of good? What good deeds have you done?"

She knew that normal wizards helped humanity. By working for *Huli* Transport, they delivered essential goods to people in distant places. They'd also helped humanity expand to the stars and prevented wars. At least according to the press releases she'd read.

Dali shot her a smile over his shoulder. "I help individuals choose their right path," he said simply. "Most magic is all about transformation."

Ren nodded. That much she knew.

"Because I can tap into a different magic, the wild energy of the universe around us, I see more patterns than a wizard can. The cards help me foretell the future."

"Really?" Ren said She wasn't sure she believed him. As far as she knew, no one could actually predict the future. Anyone who said that they could was a charlatan, not a real magic user.

"Really," Dali said. "Let me show you."

Ren thought for a few moments, paddling across the quiet bay. It still seemed more quiet this morning. Or maybe it was just her, poised to leap and unable to pick a path.

"Did Hanshu send you?" Ren finally asked. Maybe the other being had called Dali to help her.

"Who?" Dali said.

From the confusion in his tone, Ren believed that Dali didn't know Hanshu. Still, she persisted.

"He's a very powerful being who lives on Hudie Dao. He called someone last week to come and help me," Ren said. She paused, and then added, "If you do good as a warlock, and you want me to believe you, then surely you're here to fix Market Canal."

Dali nodded slowly. "All right," he said. "I can help you fix Market Canal. Then I'd like for you to become my apprentice."

"What is in it for you?" Ren asked. Nothing came for free. That was something her parents had taught her at a very young age. There was always a cost, whether it be in credits or in future favors.

"Apprentices bring a lot of power to a warlock or wizard," Dali told her. "They can be used like an extra battery of stored magical energy."

"Ah," Ren said. That made sense.

"Plus, there's the prestige of having an apprentice," Dali continued. "Particularly among warlocks. Not everyone can attract an apprentice, or keep them."

"Just keep them? Or keep them alive?" Ren asked.

"Both," Dali said. He gave her a huge smile. "And it's good that you understand the risks."

"Using more power can be tricky, as well as dangerous," Ren said. She'd learned all about that when she'd first started with *Huli* Transport. Wizards didn't always survive their training. Fewer were killed than messengers, but there was always a risk.

"Exactly," Dali said. "So you agree to become my apprentice?"

"I do not," Ren said. She spoke her words plainly, despite how she felt herself trembling to her core. "First, let's see what you can do with Market Canal. Then, let's see how well I like being your apprentice, if I'm actually suited for it, if we'll suit each other."

Dali's barking laugh echoed out over the waters again. "Fair enough. I agree to your conditions."

"And I agree to your proposal," Ren said. Though she spoke the words quietly enough, she still felt them echo out, over the water and beyond.

She'd made a choice, at least for now. Only time would tell if it was the right one.

———

DALI ARRANGED for Ren to come and pick him up later that afternoon, to take him back to Hudie Dao. He'd seemed certain that he'd be able to just fix the canal with a wave of his hand.

Ren was pretty certain that he'd fail. After all, if it were that easy, Hanshu would have already taken care of it. Plus, though Ren had told Dali that the job would require finesse, he didn't appear to understand what she was talking about.

Throughout the rest of the day, Ren raced through her deliveries. Though she paddled past the end of Market Canal more than once, she couldn't discern if there was any difference in the water. It seemed the same to her, but then again, the end of the canal hadn't had any problems.

Finally, the time for Ren's appointment with Dali came. She paddled her way up to the main pier of Market Canal to pick the warlock up. He stood at the very end of the pier, looking for her. When he saw her, he nodded and leaped down to the raft before she was ready. The raft bobbed suddenly in the water, and it took a surge of Ren's magic to steady it.

Dali peered curiously at her. "Do that again," he said.

"What, sir?" Ren asked, confused.

"Use your power on the raft," Dali instructed.

Ren wasn't certain exactly what he wanted to see, but she used more magic than normal to turn the raft around and get them headed out into the bay again.

"Huh," Dali said after a moment. "That's different."

"What do you mean, sir?" Ren asked.

"I would have thought that you'd just use your power on the raft," Dali said after a moment. "That you would have just stabilized the craft."

"Isn't that what I did?" Ren said, confused.

"No," Dali said. "Your magic affected both the raft as well as the nearby water. You work in harmony with both. You use the currents to direct the raft, don't you?"

Ren nodded. It was too much work to just push the raft over the water. After a few moments, she added, "It's a transformation. To use the existing currents instead of just pushing the raft."

"That makes sense," Dali said slowly. He peered at her, but didn't say anything more for a bit.

Finally, Ren had to ask. "Were you successful with Market Canal?"

Dali shook his head and chuckled ruefully. "I was not. My master used to tell me that my primary role as an apprentice was to teach her humility. You've started that lesson with me."

"What do you mean, sir?" Ren said, focusing on the raft instead of staring at the warlock.

"I had assumed that all I needed to do was to clear out the water. Or start the pumps on the canal going. Or something," he said. "But the problem seems more entrenched than that. It will take me a few more days. I will get the canal working again," he assured her.

"What is causing the problem?" Ren asked after a bit. "Why is the water so dead?"

"It isn't that the pumps aren't working," Dali said. "I went and inspected some of them, expecting that to be the issue, that there was a lazy mechanic or something. Or that perhaps the humans had broken the pumps and that the Seidaren hadn't sent anyone to fix them."

"Aren't the pumps maintained by humans?" Ren said, confused. While she'd known that the Seidaren had provided the equipment, she'd thought the agreement was that the humans would maintain them.

"Only to a degree," Dali said. "If the pumps break down completely, one of the Seidaren must come and fix it. The pumps use the same technology that the Seidaren use to move their cities across the water. It's a combination of magic and physics, similar to our space technology. However, their magic is so different we can't replicate it. Although…" Dali paused. "I probably have a better understanding of the Seidaren magic than most wizards. It's more similar to my own magic."

That really surprised Ren. *Huli* Transport maintained that all warlocks were evil, that the very nature of their magic was wrong. Were the Seidaren also wrong? Evil? Or just different?

"The pumps are working as expected?" Ren prompted after a few moments of quiet.

"As far as I can tell," Dali said. "I'm not an expert in these things," he added, sounding exasperated. "The water comes in. The pumps send it back out. I watched volumes of water moving. But as soon as it reached the canal, it died again."

"How did you get in to do the inspection?" Ren asked.

The pumps themselves weren't on any sort of public tour as far as she knew.

"Stole the identity of an inspector," Dali said proudly.

Ren didn't know how to respond to that. What Dali had done wasn't exactly lawful. Then again, he was a warlock. He wouldn't necessarily do *lawful*, as it were.

"Where's the problem?" Ren asked. "If the pumps are working, what is killing the water?"

"There are pumps all up and down the canal," Dali said. "I went and checked the ones starting about midway up the canal. They were operating fine. I assume that means the problem is upstream. I traveled up to the start of the delta, where the Munda River divides into the four canals. The pumps up there appear to be working as well. The water is coming into the canals as expected."

"What is killing Market Canal?" Ren said again, persistent and stubborn as only she could be.

"I don't know!" Dali said. The frustration was back in his voice. "I can't tell if it's natural or magical in nature. All I can tell is that at a certain point, the water starts to die. I couldn't even revive it, though water is sort of my specialty." He glared at her, as if she had something to do with his failure.

"The water council is aware that something is wrong with the canal," Ren said slowly, carefully trying to calm Dali. "Or at least whoever is monitoring the general message system. They are the ones who faked the numbers that are being publicly reported."

Dali nodded. "And they're probably lying to everyone who reports a problem. Not carrying the messages forward to someone who can actually do something about the problem."

"Unless it's the entire water council who's in on the conspiracy," Ren said. That had been her theory.

Dali shook his head. "It's too difficult to keep a secret

with even two people, let alone a council of seven. No, not that many people know about it. Maybe one person on the council is aware of the issue. My gut tells me it's someone outside the council who's bribed someone on the council."

"So what are you going to do next?" Ren said after a bit.

"I don't know!" Dali said. He sounded even more angry than before. "I wouldn't have agreed to your conditions if I had thought this problem was going to be so difficult."

Ren shrugged. While it might be nice to have more power or control, she wasn't about to budge or let Dali off the hook.

"Should I go with you next time?" Ren asked after a bit. After all, Hanshu had said that he'd send someone to help her with the problem. Maybe he didn't expect for whoever he sent to do all the work, though Ren wasn't sure what she could do to help.

Dali appeared to hold that opinion as well. "Why? What can you do?"

"I know water," Ren said.

"So do I," Dali said after a while. "I was born on this planet, after all. And I work with it. All the time. Both physical rivers as well as rivers of probability."

"But not these waters," Ren said stubbornly. "You didn't realize the water in the canal was dead until I pointed it out."

"True," Dali said. "You are more sensitive to the water. Maybe it would make sense for you to come along." Dali paused for a few moments. "Yes. I will request for you to ferry me up Market Canal. We will both examine the water, see if we can tell exactly where the problem is occurring."

"On my raft?" Ren asked. She couldn't keep the horror from her voice. She didn't want to be that close to the dead waters.

"Can you pilot a powered boat?" Dali said.

"I can," Ren said. "I've been trained to pilot most of them. Rent one of those."

"I'll arrange it for the day after tomorrow," Dali said.

Ren set her jaw and nodded. She would do this. It would be awful being on the dead water. But if this was how she'd be able to fix it, she would.

# TEN

Xiyi asked Ren to come into the office the following afternoon. Ren wasn't sure why. Were there more results from her testing that her boss wanted to go over?

The office looked the same as it always did, immaculately tidy, everything filed and put away. A hologram of a large, brilliant red hibiscus flower standing in a pot had been added to the corner of Xiyi's desk. It was odd. Anyone with magic could see through a hologram. It was part of the teaching protocol for messengers: filling a classroom with some real people but mostly with holograms. How quickly the messenger noticed was an indication of their power.

Ren wasn't sure of the significance of the hologram. Maybe Xiyi didn't want to bother with a real flower, as it might be messy, dropping petals or dripping water. But surely her boss could afford a better hologram, one that didn't look so fake.

Xiyi saw Ren looking at the flower. "You spotted that it wasn't real instantly, didn't you?" she asked as Ren sat down carefully on one of the uncomfortable chairs on her side of the desk.

Ren merely nodded.

"It's been educational, having it here," Xiyi said. "I've been taking bets with myself who would realize that it was fake the soonest. I hadn't imagined that you would win."

Ren wondered if it was in part her sensitivity to electricity that gave her an edge, but she wasn't about to say anything about that to her boss. She wanted to remain a messenger and not get forced into management.

"It's been brought to my attention that you've caught the attention of a warlock," Xiyi said, drawing her tablet closer across her desk. "Wang Dali."

"What do you mean?" Ren said. Her heart suddenly started pounding hard. She'd told Dali that it was against the company rules for her to fraternize with a client!

"He's requested you, you specifically, to ferry him around for the next week or so, while he's visiting Jung Wa," Xiyi said. "He'd like to set up a retainer for you, so that your only duties for the next two weeks would be to ferry him."

"Huh," Ren said. She hadn't known that was a possible service that the company would offer. Then again, she did have clients who asked for her specifically, just not for long periods of time.

"You know that the company, while it maintains a neutral position when it comes to deliveries and ferrying, does not approve of warlocks, right?" Xiyi asked.

"Why, though?" Ren asked. "Is it because their magic is so different?"

Xiyi gave Ren a wintery smile, one that was more threatening than any wizard. "I wondered if that was the problem. You shouldn't listen to Dali's lies. Warlocks are evil. Their magic is harmful. It cannot be controlled. After a while, all warlocks end up killing themselves, either through negligence or deliberately."

"Really?" Ren said. "But what about Ao Dan?"

"Who?" Xiyi asked. She seemed confused. Obviously, she hadn't been expecting Ren to do anything but fold.

"Ao Dan. He's partially responsible for the portals," Ren said stubbornly. She'd looked up the name. It wasn't listed on the *Huli* Transport site. However, Ao Dan was the subject of a great deal of speculation, particularly regarding the development of the portals. Her search had turned up a lot of hits.

Some of the sites even claimed that he was still alive.

Xiyi swiped her tablet on and typed in the name.

A voice suddenly came through the speaker. "Dao Xiyi, why are you requesting information about this individual?"

Ren sat frozen in her chair. What sort of security alert had her manager just tripped? Who was this Ao Dan?

"One of my messengers, Jung Meiren, asked about the name," Xiyi said. "It was something a client had mentioned to her."

Xiyi glared at Ren across her desk. Ren gulped. This wasn't good. Not in the least.

"This is not an individual whom you need to be concerned with," the voice went on. "Is Jung Meiren in the office with you?"

"She is," Xiyi confirmed.

"Send her to room 691 when you are finished," the voice said.

A hard silence filled the small office.

Xiyi deliberately turned off her tablet. With a wave of her hand, Ren knew that the office had suddenly become impenetrable. No one would be scrying or listening in on their conversation.

"Say nothing. Admit nothing. It was just a name you heard from a client. You don't even remember which one. And never speak of it again. Do you understand?" Xiyi's voice was hard enough to break nails.

Ren nodded.

Xiyi released the privacy spell. "So I shouldn't approve Dali's request then, correct?" she said, sounding pleasant enough.

"Instead of two weeks, just give me one day," Ren said. "So I can tell him to leave."

Xiyi gave her a warm smile. "That's completely appropriate," she said. "Thank you."

Ren left the office quickly, heading up to the sixth floor. She was certain that she was still on Xiyi's shit list. It would take time to get off of it.

Hopefully her boss wouldn't be angry enough to do something in retaliation, such as start sending Ren through portals.

---

THE OFFICE REN was led into was sterile. It reminded her in some ways of the dead water in Market Canal. Fans blew cold air down on their latest victim. The walls, the conference table, and the chairs were all white, the carpet industrial gray. The ceiling at least had a little interest, white with a slight texture to it. Ren wondered if that was to hide the camera and microphones imbedded into it (which she could spot immediately, as where electricity ran were the areas that glowed the brightest to her).

Ren waited patiently until a security officer finally found the time to come and see her. She knew that it was part of their process, to let her sit alone and "sweat." However, it would have been more effective if it hadn't been so cold. Ren found herself getting angry, not afraid.

The officer wore a black uniform that appeared cut out of the night, absorbing all the light in the room. It made him difficult to look away from. The shirt was bulky with gadgets built into the shoulders and the chest. It was probably armored as well.

Instead of a tablet or file, he wore a pair of data glasses. Ren could tell by the way his eyes shifted up, down, and to the sides, that he was looking up more information.

"Jung Meiren," the officer said. "You had a warlock for a client, recently. Wang Dali."

"I have," Ren said. She wasn't about to lie about that. It was in the company's records.

"Was that client the one who mentioned Ao Dan?"

Ren put on her best confused face. "Maybe? I don't remember. I have a lot of different clients, you know. Many of whom like to talk. Just yesterday I ferried a woman—Zuli —who spoke a mile a minute the entire time we crossed the bay. The only time she stopped talking was when we reached the pier."

Though the security officer maintained a neutral face, Ren could tell that he was upset with her reply.

"You understand that warlocks are not part of *Huli* Transport, correct?" the officer continued.

"I do," Ren said. "They're evil." She shivered. She figured she did a pretty good job at that. Not because she was scared, but because it was really fricking cold in this room.

"Your boss Dao Xiyi has denied this warlock's request for your services exclusively for the next two weeks, only granting him a single day," the officer said.

"That's correct," Ren said. "I want to tell Dali myself that I am not interested in ferrying him anymore. He can use whoever is available that day, instead of just my services. That way, the company stays neutral and maintains its promise of service to all."

Ren kept her words clear and her tone proud. While the officer would have liked her to crumble, Ren wouldn't do that. Not for anyone. She knew she was skirting the line between truth and falsehood, dancing on that edge.

But she would do as Xiyi had told her to do.

After asking a few more times who had mentioned Ao Dan's name, the security officer finally appeared to believe Ren that she just couldn't remember who she'd heard the name from. Or why she thought it was important enough to bring up to her manager. They'd just been shooting the breeze, you know? Someone had mentioned it. Xiyi had thought it was an unusual enough name to look it up.

"All right," the security officer said after a few more moments, obviously looking something else up on his data glasses. "You can go. I cannot officially ask you to report anything suspicious about what Dali says or asks for. However, a proper employee would remember that warlocks are the enemy, and any information is vital."

Ren blinked, surprised. She had realized that the company didn't like warlocks. But that they were considered the enemy was new.

"I will, sir," Ren said.

The officer stood up and allowed Ren out of the room. She didn't take a deep breath until she was finally out of the office building and back into the bright sunshine.

It would take a while, though, for the warmth to work its way through her body and to her chilled core.

What was it about warlocks that was considered so evil? And did she want to pursue such a course if it set the company against her?

---

REN PICKED Dali up on Hudie Dao the next morning. Spring rains still sprinkled the water. Ren wore a large, conical hat that only appeared to be woven out of straw. It was actually provided by the company and was completely waterproof. Ren frequently wore it during the day when the sun was too bright, as while it kept the rain off, it was still cool and allowed breezes in.

She wore her usual brown jumpsuit, which was much less of a technical marvel than her hat. It was plain cloth, and while it was water resistant, it wasn't waterproof. It covered her completely so that only her hands were exposed to the sun. She didn't like wearing gloves, though her mom sometimes despaired because Ren's hands were so rough.

Despite the warnings about warlocks, Ren continued to wear her hair as she always had. Giving it up felt too much like giving up an important part of herself. She just wouldn't do it.

Ren held the raft steady when Dali jumped down onto it. He landed lightly, probably aided by his magic.

"Would you care for an umbrella?" Ren asked, knowing that he didn't want a chair or a bench. The rain wasn't hard, but it was a steady mist.

"I'll take care of myself, thank you," Dali said.

A brief blue flash emanated from the warlock. Ren knew that he'd just set up some sort of personal shield so the rain wouldn't touch him. She suspected that he'd just done it to protect his face, hair, and hands, as the suit he wore—navy blue and impeccably tailored—probably had its own protections.

"My request for your services exclusively has been denied," he said as Ren maneuvered the raft around and headed away from the island, back to the mainland.

"I know," Ren said. "I told them to just give me a single day with you. I'm supposed to tell you that I want nothing more to do with you."

"But?" Dali said. He gave her a sly smile.

"You need fix Market Canal. And I have given you my

word that I would see if being your apprentice would suit me," Ren said seriously. "However, I have to tell you, you are going to have to be very persuasive. Though you tell me you aren't evil, the company believes that all warlocks are."

Dali nodded seriously. "I know." He sighed. "Many warlocks do turn cruel with age. Wizards can as well, but not as many do."

Cruel and lawless? That might be why the company considered them evil. And while Dali had a cruel smile, he hadn't actually been mean to her. Yet. "They also claim that your magic is unstable," Ren pressed.

"Others consider it so," Dali said. "There are sometimes…unexpected consequences. With enough training, those can be dealt with."

Ren didn't like the sound of that. What if she didn't have enough power to deal with the unexpected consequences? It sounded as though being a warlock was more dangerous than being a wizard. Even though she was facing a life of disability if she stopped now, she wasn't sure she wanted to continue.

She'd given her word, though. She would at least try it.

"What is the plan for today?" Ren asked after a while. The world seemed closed in, the mists hiding the city in front of them.

"I've rented a motorboat to take us up Market Canal," Dali said. "I expect you to pilot it. We're going all the way up to the head of the canal, see if either of us can spot something from the river that's invading the waters of the canals, polluting them. I looked before, but your sensitivity may show us something more."

Ren nodded. She'd been thinking about Hanshu's statement that they needed finesse to deal with the dead waters. "What if it is something from upriver that's coming into the canal? Wouldn't that affect all of the canals?"

"Possibly," Dali said. "But I'd like to rule out the Munda River first as the possible source."

That made sense to Ren. There wasn't much more for her to ask. So she paddled them in silence across the waters, through the mists and the rain, each settled into their own thoughts and schemes.

# ELEVEN

Ren was happy that the jetty for the rental boats was at the end of Market Canal, where it met the bay, so she wouldn't have to cross the dead waters just yet.

The boat itself was about five feet wide, so about the same as her raft, but it was considerably shorter. There was a wheel on a post in the center of the boat, as well as two seats behind that. That was it. She'd seen scooters with more storage room.

Ren hadn't driven this particular model of boat before, but she'd been trained to drive similar enough crafts that she didn't feel nervous about piloting it. It probably turned like crap and the engine wouldn't handle any waves. The only reason it wouldn't immediately capsize was because it had stabilizers built into the hull to keep it upright.

That actually made piloting it easier, as Ren wasn't going to take any chances and try going fast, or even attempt anything challenging as they puttered along.

Market Canal was wider at the end and would grow steadily more narrow, until it reached a width of thirty feet across. Ren drove them away from the dock and up the canal in the lane designated for boats going upstream. They passed more than one food boat selling hot pork buns, chicken and garlic congee, as well as hot tea and coffee to those commuting into the city that morning. In addition, several offered umbrellas as well as cheap plastic ponchos to protect people from the soft misting rain.

It surprised Ren when Dali put the boat into a bubble of protection. "We'll probably be followed today," he said grimly.

"I see," Ren said. She hadn't thought about that. Since the company didn't really care for warlocks, it made sense.

"You do realize that once we fix Market Canal, if the news of its condition gets reported widely, that I'll be blamed for causing it in the first place, right?"

"Why? Why wouldn't the actual perpetrators be held accountable?" Ren asked, shocked.

Dali's barking laugh echoed strangely in their protective bubble. "Because they can," he said bluntly. "*Huli* Transport can. Remember that."

Ren shook her head but didn't reply. They rapidly reached the area where the waters were dead. It gave her the creeps to be driving over them. She feared splashing too much, as if the drops were actually acid and would kill whatever they touched, or at the very least, suck the life out of it.

It was different than being in a cloud of electronics. Instead of biting ants, it was more like a weighted shroud, pressing her down into the canal, threatening to smother her. She found it difficult to breathe. A metallic taste clung to the air, making her jaw ache and her teeth tingle.

"The waters have changed, haven't they?" Dali asked quietly.

Ren nodded.

"I didn't feel the difference," he remarked after a bit. "At least, not as quickly as you did. I am only starting to feel it now."

That made Ren feel better actually, that perhaps she did know the waters of New Hong Kong better than he did.

They drove in silence up the canal. Ren didn't bother pointing out that there were no fishing boats on the edges of water, no people fishing from any of the private piers. It meant, though, that there had been too many mornings with no fish for them to continue. How long had this been going on? How many had reported the condition of the water to the council? How many had been lied to or silenced?

It took almost two hours to reach the far end of the canal, in part because Ren couldn't make their small craft do more than putter along. She couldn't use magic to aid their speed, as the waters were too dead—there was no current to work with or against.

The sun had finally broken through the clouds by the time they neared the canal end. Ren had hoped that the sunlight would have made her feel better, but it didn't. Instead, the air grew humid and even more oppressive. Ren found herself sweating more than usual, probably due to nerves and tension. She kept her hat on, blocking the sunlight from her eyes. The metallic taste in her mouth grew stronger. Her whole mouth prickled as if she'd been chewing foil.

Big warning signs hung above the canal, alerting pilots that the open waters were ending. Either they needed to dock their craft, or else form a line to the left to enter the locks. Dali directed Ren to the left—they were going to go through the locks and onto Munda River.

Apartment buildings rose up on either side of the canal. Despite the private jetties for the residents there, the paint on the buildings was faded and cracked, and the concrete looked strained. Ren couldn't help but shudder. She'd never be able to live someplace like that, constrained on all sides by people. There were some nice wide areas that weren't developed, parks and greenways between the buildings. However, she saw shacks there as well, lean-tos built under the trees, the poorest of the poor living there.

Would she be forced into such an existence by her sensitivities? Was that the problem with some of those living here?

Ren slowed the craft as she drove forward, though a part of her wanted to flee over the water, get out of the poisoned area and onto the fresh waters again. Even walking on land would be better than in this awful morass.

Except...there were fishing boats here. She saw young boys, shirtless with tattered pants, fishing on the edges of the water.

Were there fish here? Or were they just that desperate?

It took her a moment to shake off the overwhelming feeling of the dead water.

The waters here were mixed. It was similar to the end of the canal, where the waters from the bay came in.

She turned to look back at Dali. He had a circle of blue light cackling between his hands. She had the impression he was seeking something, like a con-artist with a crystal ball. The light emphasized the harsh lines across his face, his hawk nose and cruel lips. He struck her as the ultimate predator, with a charming veneer and the desire to suck the life out of those around him.

However, he did look up when she moved, one eyebrow raised in question.

"The waters are clearer here," Ren told him quietly.

Dali pushed his hands together, squishing the magic between them. It flattened with an explosive spark. The smell of ozone filled the air and a wave of magic washed over Ren, raising all the hairs on her arms as well as on the back of her neck. It chased away the metallic taste on her tongue, instead flooding her mouth with the warm, almost bitter taste of syrup, maybe blueberry, the sweet kind poured over shaved ice.

She shook her head. Dali grinned at her discomfort. Then he grew more serious, his eyes turning inward as he sent his own senses out, seeking the differences in the canal waters.

"Are you sure?" he asked after a few moments.

"There are fishermen here," Ren said, gesturing toward the banks. "Where the waters were completely dead, nobody fished. The people had left because there was nothing to catch."

"Or these people are that desperate," Dali said, looking around with distaste.

"The waters are more clear," Ren said stubbornly. She slowed down the craft to just above a crawl. With every passing minute, the waters grew more alive.

Only a few larger craft were in front of them, passing into the locks. As they joined the line, Dali finally nodded. "I can feel the difference," he said. He glared at her, as if it was somehow her fault.

"Do we continue? Go up into the river?" Ren asked after a few moments.

Dali thought for a few moments before he shook his head and said, "Park the boat. I want to walk up to the locks, maybe take the tour, but I suspect you're correct. The problem is in the canal water and not in the river."

Ren nodded, slipping out of line and heading toward one of the public piers to dock her tiny boat.

However, she didn't feel any relief. If the problem had been the river, then it probably would have been easier to solve. Someone else's problem, almost.

If the problem was just in the city…that meant a rot there. Corruption. A larger issue.

Ren feared that she'd shortly have to learn exactly what Hanshu meant by *finesse*.

---

REN WAS FASCINATED with the huge turbines that divided the mighty river waters into the much more tame canals, tapping the energy of the river and turning it into electricity. She'd never traveled to the locks before. While she loved the bay and the still waters she paddled across, there was a part of her that was thrilled by the rushing, powerful waters of the river. Even through the miasma brought on by all the electronics, the powerful generators stationed above the water.

Dali gave her a speculative look as they left the tour, walking slowly back to where they'd docked the boat.

"What?" Ren finally asked, aware of how defensive she sounded and not quite sure she cared.

"You and the river," Dali said after a few moments. "I think that if you ever traveled up it, you'd never leave."

Ren snorted. "Really? You think that my commitments to my family are that weak?"

He shrugged. "The river is chaotic, you know," he said after a few moments. "The waters are turbulent. It's the heart of a chaos warlock. Not an orderly wizard."

Ren stopped, stunned. "No," she said after a few moments. "A regular wizard would appreciate the strength and power found here."

Dali shook his head. "There's so much for you to learn. If only you'd allow me to teach you."

Ren peered at him, afraid that he was right. However, she didn't want to start down that path. Not yet.

"Fixing Market Canal is going to take some time," Dali said, continuing. "You should give me a day to show you your power now. Let me show you how to surf those waves."

Ren shook her head, though she was oh-so-tempted. Particularly if being a warlock was like the wild river behind her.

"Imagine a wave, thirty feet tall," Dali said quietly. "It's surging under your feet. Power sparking your skin. You're dancing at the very tip of that wave, singing, roaring, praying. The heavens above you are echoing your commands, the universe bending to your will."

Ren felt as well as saw the picture Dali painted. Out on the sea, past the calm of Baohu Bay and into the rough oceans. Huge waves that swamped boats and cities. She surfed at the top of that wave, laughing at the puny winds trying to push her around, despite their gale-like strength. There was so much power surging through her. Nothing else mattered. Not her ruined face, not her sensitivities, not even her destroyed family.

Just the dance of power. Just the sweet smell of her own sweat as she worked greater and greater magics. Just the life she could finally live, all on her own.

Dali may have been exaggerating her power, but the vision she saw was true. She could go there. Tap that wild potential inside of herself. Go her own way and not worry about being overwhelmed by modern life.

Was that really the course she wanted to take? It would require her to walk away from everything. Her family. Her job. All normal society.

Was it possible to siphon off a portion of that power? Not have the entire pie but merely a single slice? Find that place between her two dismal futures? Alien, alone, and incredibly powerful, or still human, alone, and overwhelmed?

"All right," Ren said after a few moments and the vision

had cleared, leaving her standing on the bank of the canal, the semi-dead waters in front of her. "We still need to fix Market Canal. But I'd like to tap that magic."

Dali nodded. "I know you just want to touch it, and not take it on fully. There aren't any magic users who are both lawful and chaotic. You can either be one or the other."

"I want to try," Ren said stubbornly. "It's the only path for me. That middle road between the extremes."

"You're no Buddha," Dali said disparagingly.

Ren shrugged. That wasn't about to stop her.

As they boarded the boat, she asked, "What is the next step for curing Market Canal?"

Dali sighed. "Is there a spot where the water is deadest on the canal? The bad influence is obviously weaker on either end. Let's concentrate on the middle, as it were," he said with a soft smile, "see if we can find the spot of origin."

"That's logical," Ren said, approving. She took a deep breath of the clear air, preparing herself to go back onto the dead water.

She'd hoped that since she knew what it would be like that it would be better this time. However, it was worse. It felt as though rough cloth had been wrapped around her, cutting off all her senses.

She shook her head, hating the sensation. She couldn't hear any words, but she had the siren sense of needing to end it all. Drive the craft into an oncoming boat, splinter it into shards and drown in the cold waters.

"I think it's the side of the canal we're on," Dali said, breaking through her misery. "I can sense the dead waters much more strongly on this side than I could on the other."

Ren blinked, surprised. That made sense. Why hadn't she thought of it? Oh, right, because she could barely breathe through the heat and pressure and gloom.

"Can you pull over for a moment?" Dali asked after a short while.

Ren nodded and went through the motions automatically, puttering over to a public dock, throwing a rope around one of the poles. She breathed shallowly, through her mouth. The metallic taste was back, her teeth aching. Her hands clenched and unclenched, as if she could grab hold of the blanket smothering her and push it away. Her stomach rolled queasily, and the breakfast she'd had many hours before still laid like a stone in her belly.

When Ren finally turned around, she found that Dali had conjured a map of the canal. He used a device she'd never seen before. It looked like a pointed hourglass, maybe three inches long, with what looked like ash, not sand, flowing between the two round bulbs. He projected the map from the device, and could zoom in and out by moving the device.

It wasn't a mechanical device, but a magical one, used to focus a magic user's attention. Ren would bet that it was a tool that a regular wizard could use, but she wasn't about to risk insulting the warlock by asking.

"So we're here," Dali said, using his free hand to point to a place on the map. The map suddenly displayed what looked like a satellite view of the area, showing the buildings nearby. It was cast in weird colors, yellow-brown with tinges of blue.

Ren had that surging taste of syrup again, though this time it was more of a raspberry flavor, but still with that hint of ice underneath. Was that what wild magic tasted like? She wasn't sure if it was a flavor she could get used to, or if she'd grow tired of it quickly.

Dali shortened the map, flowing up to the start of the canal. "Here's the place where the dead waters start," he said. The canal waters were tinted reddish up there, making Ren feel even more unsettled.

"The middle of the canal is roughly here," he added, rapidly traveling down the map and heading toward the center.

The area Dali reached wasn't what Ren thought of as the heart of the city. That was downstream, closer to the bay. This area was the very western edge of downtown. Instead of the fancy, expensive shops and arcades visited by tourists, it had venues that only locals would use, smaller department stores and diners, with teashops and bars scattered in between.

"You see here?" Dali said. He indicated the area slightly upstream. "That's Factoryville."

Ren had heard the name before. It referred to the area of New Hong Kong where most of the factories were located. They looked like a gray band across the map as Dali spread it out.

"None of the other shops or buildings in the area actually make use of the canals," Dali said, "except as a highway." Then he pointed to the hulking factories and expanded the map further. "See these?"

Spikes ran off the canal, little waterways that shot straight for the factories then back again. It reminded Ren of a horror vid she'd once seen, with a creature whose circulation was external, in tubes running up and down its body. What were the factories doing with the canal waters? She didn't remember any of the factories requiring water. But maybe they did. Maybe some of the equipment ran too hot, and running canal water through was the easiest (and cheapest) way to cool the machines. Or maybe there was some other process and the factory workers used the waters to wash materials.

"There aren't that many factories that use Market Canal waters," Dali confirmed. "What do you want to bet that the problem is coming from one of them?"

Ren shook her head. "That seems too easy," she said after a moment.

Dali shrugged. "Sometimes the simplest explanation is the best. Besides, if there's a problem with one of the factories, it won't actually be that easy to fix."

Ren pressed her lips together but had to nod in agreement. The factories were powerful. The managers there were comparable to the wizards at *Huli* Transport. Or perhaps with even more clout, like corporate supervisors. The factory directors controlled everything in New Hong Kong, dictating the lives of thousands.

Had one of them decided to destroy New Hong Kong? But why? It made no sense.

"We will need to trace the waters up and down the feeders," Dali said. "See if we can pinpoint the source of the poison."

"And what if we don't find anything?" Ren asked as Dali compressed the map further, rolling it up around the hourglass like a cloud-thin ribbon.

"Then we go back to the start. Develop a new theory," Dali said. He looked at her seriously. "I won't let this go," he promised her, "whether you continue this training or not."

"Why?" Ren said. That didn't seem to be in line with Dali's nature, to try to fix things when he could be spreading more mayhem.

"Whoever is destroying the canal isn't doing it to just sow chaos," Dali said. "This is something more than that."

Ren nodded. She appreciated the distinction he was making. This wasn't chaos for the sake of chaos. This was destruction, something that went beyond.

She started the boat up again before she untied it. They quickly began puttering down the river again.

If they were dealing with corrupt factory directors, well, that might call for the level of *finesse* that Hanshu was talking about. Particularly if one had managed to bribe someone on the water council.

But Ren couldn't think about that.

All she could do was swallow her fear of actually having to enter a factory, then surviving the onslaught of light, noise, electricity, and everything else sure to overwhelm her there.

# TWELVE

Ren couldn't pilot their small boat up the side canal to the factories: No boats were allowed on those waters. Plus, they were too narrow and shallow for even the tiny boat she was currently driving.

So Ren and Dali were forced to walk up the side canal. Though there were fences with huge signs declaring "No Admittance" and "No Trespassing," Dali ignored all of them, leading her through the gates as if they were not only unlocked but wide open.

He seemed less reserved than she'd seen him before, approaching giddy. Maybe it was breaking the law that made him so happy. He was the epitome of chaos, after all.

Would she, someday, have the same disdain for common courtesy and signage? Would she delight in trespassing, going where she wasn't supposed to? Walking in the forbidden areas made her deeply uncomfortable. She was a good girl, as she liked to remind herself.

However, she was traveling with a warlock, specifically after she'd been warned away by her employer. Worse, she was a co-conspirator to possibly taking down one of the factory directors. There wasn't much justification she could lay out for that. She'd been taught to respect her elders and her superiors.

But if the director wasn't doing the right thing…

Ethically, she should follow the rules. Morally, she needed fix the canal.

"What do the waters feel like here?" Dali asked, breaking in on her considerations.

They'd walked about a hundred yards up from the main canal. They were in a section that was clear and flat, surrounded by warehouse buildings. There were actually two of the smaller offshoots, running side by side, one into the factory and the other one out.

Ren knelt down next to the artificial canal. Or at least it felt more artificial to her than any of the four main waterways. The offshoots were contained in solid concrete, while the other canals had accumulated enough mud on the bottom of them for plants to grow and for fish to live in them.

The path beside the two canals was like one of the sidewalks downtown, wide enough for two people to walk abreast, but not three. Ren assumed that the factory had specialized equipment for dealing with the canals, smaller machines that would run up and down the side. The concrete itself wasn't like the variety used with the poorer apartment blocks she'd seen earlier that morning. Instead, it contained an element that caused all dirt and grime to slide right off. The canals themselves probably didn't have to be cleaned very often as the material that held them wouldn't allow dirt to grow.

Dali had stopped between two of the monitoring stations that perched every fifty yards or so, looking like black ticks clinging to the sides of the canals, bathing in the waters. Ren forced herself to get closer, to actually kneel down next to the canal and get near the water.

It stank. Not in a literal sense, but emotionally and psychically. An unseen cloud rose from it, attacking her senses, drowning her in an awful foulness.

Ren still drew closer. She first focused on the canal nearest to them, the one shooting water into the factory. It was so horrible. She found herself gagging. So much worse than merely being surrounded by electricity.

But the canal leaving the factory was marginally more awful. The first one made her want to strangle the first person she found who was responsible for the condition of the waters.

The second made her want to kill herself rather than suffer with such water beside her.

Ren rose up, her eyes watering as if she'd been sniffing fresh onions, her stomach rolling. She nearly retched. The world grew dim for a moment as she gulped fresh air.

"That one," she said. Her hand shook as she pointed to the far canal. "It's worse." Her voice cracked as she said the words. She felt as though she was pronouncing the doom of the factory itself.

Which perhaps she was.

"That line comes directly from Mutashimo Electronic Works," Dali said, calling up his map briefly. "No other factory feeds into it."

"What do they make?" Ren asked, curious. She knew that all the factories specialized in different types of parts. Some worked with the unique minerals mined on Jung Wu. Some made toys or consumer goods. Others did more technical work.

"Uhmmm…" Dali paused while he looked up the

factory. "Specialized electronic parts used primarily in spaceships, space stations, and such. There's nothing here about why they use the canal waters as part of their processing."

"What about the monitoring equipment?" Ren said, indicating the little machines on either side. "Is it giving fake results?"

She didn't like the gleam that came to Dali's eyes.

"Let's find out, shall we?" he said. He stepped closer to the canal and knelt down. "God, that's wretched," he said. Then he shook his head and placed his hands on the edge of the water.

Ren felt rather than saw the surge of magic that flowed out. Her hair stood up on the back of her neck, and a warm wash of energy passed over her.

Magic and electricity didn't work well together—something she'd had to live with every day of her life.

The surge of wild magic that Dali sent out was deliberately unfriendly to anything electronic. The monitors on either side of them started smoking. Ren watched the ones both upstream and downstream of them pop one by one.

Then the concrete Dali rested his hands against suddenly melted.

Ren stifled a gasp and stepped back.

Dali cursed, using language worse than that used in the vids that her brothers had shown her once, things her parents wouldn't approve of.

The warlock's hands were now trapped in the concrete. All of the area around him was starting to melt, drawing him down into the ground.

He wouldn't be able to escape if he didn't get out soon. However, no matter how he strained, he appeared caught, like a fish on a line.

Ren wasn't sure what to do. Her first instinct was to splash water on the problem. Except that the water was dead. If Dali had any open wounds it would get in and infect him in ways worse than any plague.

So Ren followed her second instinct, which was to physically lift Dali up and out of harm's way. Her muscles strained across her back as she took on his weight. But she spent her days paddling, lifting passengers, even picking up her raft. Plus, the warlock was lighter than he looked. Though he was a tall man, he was scrawny.

He let his magic do all his work for him, so he had no muscle tone.

It helped that Dali was stuck in the position he'd been in, crouched down and contained. It made it easier for Ren to muscle him out of the way.

Once Dali was no longer touching the concrete in that area, he started to recover. His muscles loosened, and after a few more moments he was able to straighten up.

Ren kept an eye on the area of the concrete that had started melting. As soon as Dali was no longer in the area, it appeared to harden up again.

However, the impression of someone kneeling there was still apparent in the hard surface. She could easily make out his knee prints, as well as his handprints.

Would the police be able to take fingerprints from the surface? Or maybe acquire DNA?

While Dali recovered, Ren splashed the dead water up on the affected area. As she'd suspected, the residual magic collided with the dead waters, sending up a pillar of hissing steam.

"We need to go. Now," Ren said, starting to hustle Dali back down the way they'd come. "Cover us."

Dali waved his hands and mumbled something in a language Ren didn't understand.

Nothing happened.

Dali cursed again and then said the single word, "Hide," in Cantonese. The power behind the word made Ren's hair blow away from her face for an instant in an unseen wind.

However, they were now hidden from all eyes, of that she was certain. The world lost some of its color due to the thickness of the protective bubble. Sound faded as well.

With Ren supporting at least half of Dali's weight, they made their way back to the boat. Only after they'd taken off and had puttered downstream for several minutes did Ren bother asking, "So what the hell was that?"

She risked a glance over her shoulder at her passenger, who appeared to be slowly recovering. The color was nearly back in his cheeks, though his eyes still seemed hooded.

"Unexpected consequence of wild magic," Dali said grimly.

"How would you have gotten out of there if I hadn't been there?" Ren asked, suddenly very worried.

Was that why *Huli* Transport was so against warlocks? Because of those unexpected consequences that might suddenly kill not only their powerful magic user but everyone around him or her?

"Trust me," Dali said. He gave a heavy sigh. "I would have gotten out. The guards couldn't have held me."

"And what if they'd just decided to shoot you?" Ren said.

"Would have been the best outcome possible," Dali said.

She could hear the unrepentant grin in his voice.

"I could have used the power of the explosive to free myself, blow my body to the side, and then I could have disappeared," Dali continued.

Ren nodded slowly. While she didn't really understand the mechanics of the magic, she believed that Dali hadn't thought he was in any trouble.

Did she really want to deal with those sorts of consequences? Even if it meant not being so sensitive?

"Those sorts of consequences don't happen that often," Dali said, trying to reassure her. "And there are measures you can take to direct them away from yourself."

Ren wasn't sure she believed him, but she still nodded.

"Call in sick tomorrow," Dali commanded. "That way I can show you."

Ren grimaced. She did want to learn more. Even with the possible consequences.

Besides, since she didn't have much power, the consequences would be less, right?

"I cannot just call in sick," Ren said after a bit. "My supervisor would be suspicious, especially if I did it tomorrow. My day off is the day after tomorrow. Is that good enough?"

She winced at the barking laughter that followed. Though Dali wasn't cruel every minute of every day, that laugh of his showed more of his true nature.

"Teaching me my place, eh?" Dali said. "You remind me of myself when I was an apprentice, not immediately leaping to the beck and call of my master."

Ren merely nodded. She'd been faulted often enough by her parents for the exact same behavior. However, Ren spent enough time on her own, out on the waters, fighting the waves and the elements, that she wasn't about to bend for just anyone.

Her mom had told her that she had a stubborn streak wider than Baohu Bay. Dad had commented on her still waters. Combined, they made her unmovable when she wanted to be.

Dali finally sighed. "We will meet the day after tomorrow. I will take you up into the hills, a place where no one else will be, to show you how much power you could have, the magic you could be tapping into. You were born to dance on the wild waves of magic, not follow the strict lines others have set down."

Ren gulped but said, "All right."

What if Dali was wrong? What if she wasn't actually that strong?

Or worse, what if he was right?

## THIRTEEN

The day that Ren was to accompany Dali up into the hills dawned bright and clear, the summer heat starting to make its presence known even that early in the morning. She'd told her family that she'd been called into work for an emergency. It had happened in the past, though not often, one of her clients insisting that she alone ferry them across the bay.

She assured her parents that she'd be back as soon as she could, letting them believe it would be a single ferry ride. However, she knew that she'd miss most of the day with her family.

Once a month, the entire family gathered together at her eldest brother's house—her grandparents, her brothers, her cousins, the in-laws, everyone. Her eldest brother actually lived in a separate house instead of in an apartment. The house had a yard and everything.

No one else in the family could afford such a place. Then again, Zangan hadn't been able to afford it either. Everyone in the family had contributed—her grandparents and parents giving the most—so that the family would have a place to get together over the years.

Ren loved her family, and would miss seeing everyone today, as she was pretty certain that she wouldn't arrive at the gathering until very late in the afternoon, after things had wound down and many of the people had left. However, she also had to admit that spending a day out in nature, away from all people, wasn't the worst thing she could imagine.

The sun bore down hard on Ren as she paddled out across the bay on her flat skiff. She wore her uniform, as she'd had to get dressed in it before she left for the day. However, she couldn't just "borrow" her familiar raft, as she wasn't actually on official company business.

More boats were on the water than she'd expected. Then again, most people had the day off. Ren used her magic to get her out of the way an oncoming boat more than once. The electricity flowing from the private boats was much less than from one of the ferries. Was that just because the engines were so much smaller? Or was it something specific with the ferries? Ren wasn't sure.

She piloted her way to Shan Dao, the island with the most peaks. While New Hong Kong was practically flat all the way across the city, with only a few hills and valleys, many of the islands were more rocky.

Shan Dao was one of the smaller islands. It was teardrop shaped, with the point facing a northeast. No one lived there permanently. The Seidaren declared it a nature reserve, though it didn't have the flocks of butterflies the other reserves did. They did allow the humans to build paths through the woods and up into the hills.

Two public piers jutted out of a southwest section of the island. There were trails that circumnavigated the island, as well as a few that went into the hills.

The public piers were intentionally small, so that not many people could be on the island at the same time. While fancier yachts would anchor themselves in the bay and had their own small boats to ferry them to and from the island, most people needed to tie their boats to one of the crowded public piers.

No one would untie a boat already docked, as that was considered incredibly rude. Plus, there were attendants to make sure that sort of thing didn't happen. By midmorning, Ren knew that the temptation would be strong, and a line of boats would be floating a few feet away, waiting for someone to leave so they could dock.

Ren was early enough to get a good berth. The attendant at the dock looked at her curiously after she'd paid her docking fee, though Ren wasn't about to say anything.

She knew what he wanted to ask. What was a messenger doing, coming to an unpopulated island?

Then again, the gods could appear anywhere.

Ren pulled on her backpack, which held not only bottles of water but her lunch, an unappetizing protein drink that was the best she could manage at the last minute.

Dali awaited Ren at the end of the pier. At least he wasn't wearing one of his incredibly expensive suits. Instead, he was outfitted in specialty hiking clothing, starting with lightweight slacks, dove gray in color, which would wick away sweat and yet still be water resistant, lightweight and comfortable but impervious to thorns. Of course, he wouldn't wear something as pedestrian as a T-shirt, but instead had on a matching shirt and vest. He didn't bother with a hat, probably confident that his magic would protect him from the constant heat and light of the sun. He did have on dark shades that hid his eyes but his smile was still cold and cruel.

"Good morning," Dali said in a triumphant tone.

What, had he expected Ren to not show up? Though she'd had second thoughts, she would do that. Not yet. She needed to find a better way, so she wouldn't end up a burden to her family and everyone around her.

Or did he believe that what he showed her would be so miraculous that she couldn't help but immediately pledge her undying support to him? She'd known a few men like that.

Ren gave Dali a bland smile instead of the giggling snort she felt echoing deep inside her.

"This way," Dali said, turning and walking away from the quiet waters and up the path toward the shade of the trees.

Rocks crunched under Ren's shoes. She'd worn heavier ones that day, the ones with the covered toes that she generally only wore during the worst of the winter rains. The forest loomed ahead of them. She was already regretting her decision to come. It was going to be muggy and closed in up ahead. She spared a glance back over her shoulder, at the wide-open waters of the bay. Already, a stream of boats was making their way toward the island.

Hopefully they would be finished soon, and someone who would actually enjoy these trees could dock.

In the meanwhile, Ren swallowed her fear and marched forward.

---

Normally, none of the insects on Jung Wa bothered the humans. There weren't mosquitos or ticks or any other sort of insect that recognized humans as food.

However, the woods held gnats, who appeared to enjoy flying into Ren's one eye that she used to look out on the world with, or who buzzed around her ear with a whine that set her teeth on edge.

Without the gnats, Ren might have enjoyed the woods. Perhaps. Maybe. The problem was that the day was hot and humid, and no breezes blew under the trees. She enjoyed being in the shade—it was a different experience for her, as she was so used to the sun all day long.

But the air was wet and difficult to breathe. Strange birds shrieked at her from far above, accusing the two of them of trespassing. The smell was different as well, like dry baked leaves mingled with wet soil and moss. She tasted her own sweat as she walked, though her uniform kept her comfortable, wicking the moisture away.

Dali had led her confidently along the dirt path under the trees for an hour, the climb steady but not steep. Then he left the trail and struck out under the trees on his own.

Ren had difficulty following him at first. He obviously used magic to make it easier for him to walk through the underbrush. But how?

After a while, Ren got the hang of it. It was like propelling herself across the water. She just had to find the current, as it were. The leaves and branches preferred bending in one direction than another.

It felt as though she was walking along the path that strong winter winds would take through the trees. When she followed that, she was fine.

Dali paused for a moment and pulled one of the water bottles from his belt to take a sip. Ren did the same, breathing in the quiet of the trees around them.

It wasn't the same as the quiet of the waters. The trees were much louder, always talking with each other. A plethora of insects crawled among their roots, rustling in the mulch. Loud birds called to each other from the branches. Even the wind wasn't quiet. Though the forest held a type of peace that Ren recognized, if wasn't as familiar or as comfortable.

Dali wore his shades, hiding his eyes, even though there wasn't any bright light.

Did he honestly believe that hid his emotions? His mouth was far too mobile for him to do that. If he really wanted to deceive anyone, he would be better off with a scarf covering his nose and mouth, leaving his eyes clear.

He obviously felt a great satisfaction with Ren. And he was looking forward to whatever was coming next. The smugness of his smile didn't surprise Ren at all, reminding her of a fisherman coming in off the bay with a huge haul of rare fish.

Did he also seem to smell profit coming off her? She suspected so, though she didn't understand why Dali believed that she could make him rich.

But she didn't say anything, didn't question him. She was here to learn what he had to show her, not engage in petty debates.

With a nod, as if he understood her impatience, Dali put away his water bottle and started forward again. After another hour or so, they emerged from under the trees and into a natural meadow.

Ren blinked, then took a deep breath, welcoming the bright sunlight and open air. The meadow was at least twice as long as her parents' houseboat, and maybe three times as wide. She was surprised at how high they'd climbed. They looked down on the bay beneath them, the boats in the distance merely black spots. They were facing the northeast now, having traversed across the center of the island and come out on the other side.

"Let's eat here," Dali said. "Then we'll start."

Ren nodded. She wasn't that hungry, which was surprising, given how long she'd walked. Then again, she wasn't necessarily looking forward to her meal.

"Is that what you brought?" Dali said, sounding disparaging when Ren pulled out the bottle of her energy drink.

"It was all I could pick up, sneaking away as I did," Ren said. She thought longingly about the gathering she was missing, the pineapple fried rice that was her grandmother's specialty, the tender steamed pork buns her sister-in-law made, even the grilled ribs and spicy sauce that middle brother made that were generally too salty.

"Couldn't you have brought some crumbs?" Dali asked. "Conjured yourself a meal?"

Ren shook her head. While she had enough power to do that sort of transformation, changing a few grains of rice into a heaping bowl full, she probably would have destroyed the bowl that held her meal in the process. Plus, she never found magically created food to be satisfying, long term.

It filled her mouth, but not her belly or her soul.

Dali nodded, his mouth in a line of firm disapproval.

Too bad. He'd known what he was getting into when he'd started considering her as a possible apprentice—a poor messenger never likely to move up the ranks to either wizard or manager.

Dali created his own food—a bamboo-leaf wrapped rice ball, filled with garlicky chicken pieces, along with a pickled sweet pepper.

Ren opened the protein drink and took a swig. It wasn't that bad. She did try to add just a trickle of her own magic to it, sweetening it up. Of course, she went too far. She grimaced at the taste, as if she was drinking straight lemon-lime syrup, the kind used with shaved ice.

Wait a minute. That flavor was familiar.

Though Dali projected an air of innocence, looking straight ahead, Ren knew that he'd added his magic to her drink as well. No wonder it was too sweet!

Was he trying to make it taste better? Or to get her to beg for some of his crumbs?

Ren took another cautious sip of her beverage.

It really was overly sweet, bad enough to make the back

of her teeth ache and her tongue curl. The taste would linger for the rest of the afternoon, turning her stomach as well.

She continued to stubbornly drink it, knowing that Dali was watching her without staring at her. He maintained a bland expression looking out over the meadow.

They sat for a while after they'd finished their respective lunches. The grass they sat on was brown in patches, the spring rains long behind and the summer heat drying everything out. Far beneath them, the bay waters turned a deep blue, reflecting the sky. Ren almost wished for the shade of the trees as the sun continued to bake them.

Finally, Dali turned to look at her. "Are you ready?" he asked.

Ren shrugged. "As ready as I can be," she said. She didn't really know what to expect. Was this about her future? This wild magic Dali promised? Or would she fail at this as well?

No time like the present to find out.

# FOURTEEN

IT SURPRISED Ren that Dali led her back under the trees. She'd assumed that they'd stay in the open meadow, that it would be easier to control any of the "unexpected consequences" in a clear area.

However, Dali didn't walk far. A small spring trickled in front of them, along with another open space. It wasn't very large—maybe five feet long, and only a few feet across. It was much cooler, though, and Ren loved the sound of the water. Dappled light splayed across the soft dirt all around her. Boulders rested nearby, a natural hiding spot for the more shy creatures as they approached the spring.

"Ahh…sit there," Dali said, gesturing for Ren to climb one of the larger rocks, about three feet up.

Ren scrambled up, the cool stone rough but welcome against her sweaty palms. She wasn't going to be comfortable for long—the rock was hard and she couldn't find a smooth surface to rest against—but she would sit without fidgeting for as long as she could.

"Wild magic means tapping into the wild spaces inside your heart," Dali said seriously, taking on a lecturing tone.

"Everyone has them. Just most either deny them, or have them trained out of them." He paused, then asked, "What is the wildest thing you've ever experienced?"

That was easy. Ren couldn't help but smile. "Winter storms, two years ago," she said. Two of the weather satellites had been disabled due to a sun flare, less than a day before a huge storm system hit New Hong Kong. The winds had been incredible, shrieking with fury as they poured through the city. Rain had lashed down, stinging like needles. Hail had pelted every surface, some of it as large as the jawbreaker candies that children ate, breaking windows that were made of glass as well as denting wooden roofs.

Some people who had foolishly not sought shelter immediately had been killed, beaten down and drowned by the harsh storm.

Ren had been on the houseboat with her parents, riding out the worst of it. Her parents had wanted her to huddle with them in the hull, hidden away from the fury of the winds.

But Ren had found that she couldn't breathe in the closed-in space. Instead, she'd gone back up to her room and laid on her bed, relishing the sound of the winds howling and the thunder of the rain crashing down.

She'd never admitted to anyone how much the storm had thrilled her. Everyone she knew had been scared by it, while she'd felt energized.

She'd barely admitted even to herself how the storm had made her want to get up and dance like a crazed thing around her room.

The smile Dali gave her was even more smug than before. "Good. I told you, you were a natural."

Ren merely shrugged. She knew she was different than most. That didn't mean she was actually a chaos warlock.

"Close your eyes. Take yourself back to that storm.

Imagine those winds. Can you hear them howling? Raging? Blowing with fury all around you?"

Ren did as Dali requested, imagining herself back on her bed on the houseboat, listening to the sound of the storm all around her. How those winds made her heart beat quickly, pounding in her chest, as if daring her to get up and defy them. She tasted fear as well as excitement, sour and sweet alternately coating her tongue. The energy of the storm caused all the hairs on her arms to raise up, sending waves of chicken-flesh all across her skin.

"Good, good," Dali said. His voice sounded closer, but Ren resisted the urge to open her eyes to see. "Now, imagine the storm is in you. It's starting to trickle down your throat, slowly sliding under your skin."

Ren wanted to deny the storm entrance. It would tear her to pieces! She couldn't do that. She couldn't allow it access.

"No, no, not all of it, not all at once," Dali said. She felt his hand enclose her wrist. "Just a piece of it. Just a little at a time. Feel my fingers squeezing your arm. That's the only place the wind can come in."

Too late. The storm that had already invaded.

She struggled to shut it off and start again.

Sweat broke out across her back as she fought to close herself off. The winds turned into the familiar sensation of biting ants, stinging her skin, only now from the inside, as if her blood was no longer smooth but spiky. She shook her head, fighting back, closing down all her senses.

"Just focus on my touch," Dali told her.

His voice seemed far away now. She could feel his strength, how hard he gripped her arm. She would have bruises there in a few days.

Was she fighting him? Was that why he held on so tightly? When she thought about it, she realized her own arms were flailing, without her conscious input.

Served him right if she bopped him in the nose.

The snicker of amusement that thought brought enabled Ren to come back into her own space and force the wild winds out.

They didn't get to take over. She would *not* allow anyone or anything that sort of access.

She floated in the quiet of her own head, her breathing calming from panting back to normal.

"Good, good," Dali murmured. "Now, try again."

Ren thought she nodded, but she wasn't sure.

Instead of starting in the middle of the storm, she placed herself back on her raft, in the middle of the empty bay, all the water surrounding her, instead of being closed in by the houseboat.

Now, she could let the winds in. Just a trickle at a time. The smooth breeze that came as the sun crested the horizon and started its climb into the sky. The exhale that the sky gave when the temperature finally started to diminish as the sun left its throne. Night winds that sang of distant places, carrying strange scents of faraway islands.

Starting with the winds of the storm had been too much, particularly for her fragile control. Of course, Dali had wanted her to start with the biggest, baddest event she could recall.

He wouldn't be satisfied with anything less.

That quiet giggle Ren swallowed kept her tethered, more than his fingers on her wrist.

Ren knew that Dali wanted her to keep going, maybe get back to the wild storm winds. She also knew that more wind wasn't the answer, at least not for her. Instead, now she began to let the waves in. The quiet eddies that struck the piers on the far side of the bay. The wake that lapped against her raft when she crossed paths with a bigger boat. The way the houseboat rocked during a storm, the waves tame but more turbulent.

Even the quiet trickle of the nearby stream.

None of it was ordered. Ren recognized that. It was all of a chaotic nature, though a much less violent sort than Dali exalted in.

She also recognized that the waves and the winds were of a completely different nature than the ordered places already laid down in her soul, carefully reinforced by the magical training that *Huli* Transport had given her.

She basked for a while in her quietness, feeling the fullness of the new magic, how it wanted to supplant the neat paths. It wouldn't be content growing wild in the spaces in between.

Dali had been right. She couldn't have both, not at the same time. Carefully, she released the winds and the waves, letting them seep out of her skin, her muscles relaxing though she hadn't remembered tensing them.

Finally, Ren opened her eyes. She felt…full. So many things had come into her life, into her soul. She stared at the small stream just a few feet away. She didn't remember lying down on the rock, but she was on her back, stretched out uncomfortably.

It took her a few deep breaths before she could push herself up, seated again on the rough rock. She'd been there long enough that it no longer felt so cold under her. She looked up. The sky was darker. It was late afternoon. They'd been there for hours.

Dali gave her a questioning look. "Well?" he asked. He obviously wasn't certain what she'd just done, as it hadn't been in line with his expectations in the least.

Ren sighed. "You were right," she said, not needing to look up to see his greedy grin. "Chaotic magic is more natural to me."

She sighed again.

"I sense there's a 'but' coming," Dali said after a few moments.

Again, was he expecting her to leap into his arms and declare undying love or something? Ren couldn't help but snort a little, at least inside.

"But…" Dali prompted.

"But even with a different type of magic, I still have so little control," Ren said.

Dali nodded thoughtfully. "Chaos magic isn't about control. Not like lawful magic."

"You still need some level of control," Ren said stubbornly. "You saw what happened at the start."

Dali had to nod. "I will not lie to you and assure you that I can teach you that control. That is not my forte. Just like the finesse you think is necessary to fix Market Canal does not come naturally to me."

Ren was impressed. She had expected the chaos warlock to lie. But then again, he hadn't lied to her yet, as far as she knew. Maybe honesty could be more destructive to the carefully maintained lines in her society.

"So what is next?" Ren asked.

Dali looked thoughtful. "I would like for you to try to access the chaos magic again. Maybe with practice you can get better."

Ren shrugged. "It will be difficult for me to take the time off," she said. "I can't just miss my family gatherings every week."

Dali nodded. "I can create a magical training room that we can both use instead. You'd be able to access it from anywhere, even your room on the houseboat. You'd lose some sleep, but no one would have to know that you weren't there."

Ren hesitated. Did she really want to grant a chaos

warlock access to her bedroom? And would she actually have the control to be able to access such a space without blowing the doors off?

"I give you my word that I wouldn't take advantage of your trust," Dali said. "Not until you ask me to," he added with a leer.

Ren couldn't help but roll her eyes. He was so arrogant! She supposed that other women might find that charming. It just struck her as boastful, not engaging.

"We would have to practice at first, making sure I could access such a place," Ren said slowly.

"Then you agree?" Dali said.

"I do not," Ren said firmly.

Dali just grinned at her. He was always going to be pushing at her boundaries, wasn't he?

Fine. He'd soon learn just how firmly she could hold on.

She had a streak of stubbornness as wide as the bay and filled with quiet.

"We need to make sure that I can access such a training room without destroying the doors or blowing it to pieces by accident," Ren said firmly.

Dali sobered slightly. "You would think that such a lack of control would be a source of great power. But it can be a hazard, can't it?"

Ren shook her head. Had he really proposed this potential apprenticeship without understanding that? Then again, he'd probably thought that his teaching would turn her head so that it wouldn't matter.

"It's why I'm a messenger, and not a wizard," Ren said, trying to spell everything out. "I have to assume that being a messenger is my place in life, that I won't ever have enough control for more."

Dali shook his head. "You should have more."

Ren shrugged and slid off the rock, finding her feet. The

earth actually felt good, solid, something to push against. She shook off Dali's solicitous support and staggered over to the stream.

Unable to bend over, Ren fell to her knees and stuck her hands deep into the water. The coolness of it shocked her and she gasped.

But it cleared her lungs of water, and quieted the winds that still seemed to be circling closer and closer, wanting to burst into her body and steal her soul.

She splashed the cold water against her face, feeling it trickle down her neck. She shivered as it went down her spine, but she also sat up straighter, feeling as if she was coming back to herself.

When she pushed herself up to standing, she saw that Dali's lips were pursed together, obviously curious about what she was doing.

He didn't understand that she'd needed to center herself. He didn't have the solid core that she did. He walked on the waves, only really comfortable on the water and not on the earth.

Ren nodded to herself as they started making their way back to the bay and the public piers. While perhaps the chaotic magic did suit her better than the ordered lawful paths she already followed, she had to wonder if perhaps she needed a different teacher.

# FIFTEEN

REN AGREED to meet with Dali the following evening after her last delivery. As her schedule was always so varied, her parents, and more importantly, *Huli* Transport, wouldn't know that she was meeting up with him.

Therefore, it surprised Ren when it turned out that her midmorning ferry across the bay was Dali. He was using a different name, as well as a disguise: that of a much older, frail man, bent over and relying on a cane to shuffle his way up to the edge of the pier.

Ren hadn't discovered that it was Dali until she'd gotten close enough to pick him up and deposit him gently on her raft. She'd already set up a chair for the elderly gentleman for his trip across the bay.

Even getting close enough to pick up the man, Ray hadn't seen through the disguise. But Dali couldn't hide his scent, and she'd sweated enough with him the day before to instantly recognize it.

The watery eyes that peered out blearily glanced at her when she stiffened. He gave her a broad wink. Ren relaxed, though she did consider dropping him on his ass.

Instead, she gently placed him in the waiting chair, treating him with the utmost respect that a person his age engendered.

It didn't surprise her when a sudden flash of blue danced out over the water, encasing the raft in a protective bubble that none could pierce.

He didn't speak to her until they were well away from the dock and everyone else. "Tricked you, didn't I?" he said, straightening up in his seat.

"You did," Ren admitted. "Why the disguise?"

"*Huli* sent its agents after me," Dali admitted. "They'd like for me to move on. They didn't have the strength to force the issue. This time. Next time, they'll bring more."

"Oh," Ren said. She hadn't realized that the company would actually persecute warlocks.

"My brother's strong arm can only reach so long," Dali said after another few moments. "Eventually, I'll wear out his welcome as well."

"I see," Ren said, though she didn't.

Dali sighed. "My brother will protect me as long as he can. At least as long as our dear mother still breathes. Once she's dead, all bets are off. At that point, I really need to be someplace else."

"I'm sorry," Ren said. Then again, family was always difficult.

"It's all right. I chose the forbidden path. Mother doesn't understand. She just wants her darling boys to get along," Dali said, his voice turning sour and bitter.

Ren didn't know what to say or suggest, though she didn't think that it was right for different schools of magic to tear apart families.

Then again, she understood better why the company was so against warlocks now. Their magic was the antithesis of what *Huli* stood for. It was uncontrollable to a certain extent. Unpredictable. Stronger, yes. But more deadly, too.

Trying to distract Dali, Ren asked, "What are you up to today?"

"I figured a boat ride would be the perfect time to test whether or not you can access a training room," Dali said seriously as he stood up, shedding his disguise. "That way, if there is an accident, it can happen here, where there aren't any other people nearby and you can't really blow anything up."

Ren nodded. There was the chance of drowning, but that would only happen if she was knocked unconscious before she went under the water. While she could destroy the raft by accident, it might take more power than she was capable of, as it was made out of such a tough plastic.

And she'd have to trust that Dali could protect himself against her.

"All right," Ren said, agreeing.

"Hand me the paddle," Dali said, stretching out his hand.

"Just don't lose it," Ren warned. She found herself surprisingly reluctant to hand her paddle to anyone. It wasn't anything special, but she'd used it for so long. It felt as though her hands had shaped it, though she knew that wasn't possible, given the nature of the material it was made out of.

Ren made herself reach forward, handing Dali the paddle.

He strengthened the plastic, then lengthened the paddle until it was over five feet long and could hang off of each side of the raft. Instead of a handle, it now had a paddle blade on both ends.

Dali placed the paddle down carefully at the rear of the raft. It began to paddle the boat on its own, dipping into one side than the other. It didn't move much, but the steady sound of the paddle dipping into and out of the water instantly soothed Ren.

She just hoped he could reverse the transformation, that her paddle wouldn't hold the strain of his magic forever.

Dali stood up in the middle of the raft, and had Ren stand just behind him. Then he sketched a doorway with his hands. Brilliant white light streamed from his fingertips, then remained hanging in the air, the doorway evident. The space between the bright outline started filling in, until a gray door hung in the air before them.

Ren had never seen such magic before. Then again, she didn't regularly hang out with wizards or warlocks. When she sniffed, she smelled hints of ice, apple, as well as that sweet syrupy taste from before.

He looked over his shoulder at her. "Give me your hand," he said. He reached out and wrapped his fingers around her wrist, the one that was still sore from the other day.

Ren resisted. While Dali was a stronger magician, she was quite possibly stronger physically. It would be quite a struggle for him to get her to do anything physically.

"Why do you want my hand?" Ren said when Dali gave an exasperated sigh and let go.

"I want you to feel the door, to impress your psyche on it," Dali said. "I wasn't going to hurt you."

"I know. But you can't just do things. You need to ask and explain first, if you want me to learn," Ren said.

The wave of anger that bounced off of Ren surprised her. "That isn't how it's done," Dali said tensely.

Ren shrugged. She didn't care. She wasn't about to be an ordinary apprentice, do everything just because he expected it of her.

Finally, Dali relented. "Humility. Gotcha." He gave her the ghost of a smile. "And that is the other reason why warlocks take on apprentices. So that they might learn as well."

Ren knew that wasn't why Dali had wanted to take her on, but she was willing to let his statement slide.

"Now, hold out your hand, then place your palm firmly against the center of the door," Dali instructed, standing to the side so that Ren could complete the movement on her own, without him touching her.

Ren slowly reached out. At first, it felt as if she was reaching through a miasma of electricity, her skin sparking and stinging. But then she remembered the winds and water from the day before, the quiet that she'd found even at the center of the turbulence, and the fog dissipated. The energy flowed with her skin instead of against it.

The door felt cold under her fingertips, as if the solid surface was coated in ice. She recognized it as coming from Dali. That was his signature, as it were. The cold was supposed to keep everyone else out.

How could she make an impression against that?

Ren felt the cold starting to take over, sliding up from her palm and reaching for her wrist.

She couldn't allow it to go any further. No, what she needed to do was to melt an impression of her palm print in the ice.

It reminded her of the concrete from a few days before, the solid surface melting, but retaining an impression of Dali kneeling.

Ren felt the strength of the sun at her back, and started trickling that through her palm. The warmth at her back fought the coldness under her hand.

What, had Dali thought it would just take him placing her palm on the door for this to work? What was he thinking?

Or would it have been easier with him there? To force the

ice to cooperate, rather than Ren having to fight it on her own?

It didn't matter. Ren was determined to win.

She pushed her heat down her arm. For once, she was able to maintain that slow trickle instead of a huge blast.

Maybe she could get the hang of this. Just a little bit of something, instead of everything all at once.

As she felt her hand start to sink into the ice, she glanced at Dali to give him a quick smile.

He looked worried, not pleased.

"What's wrong?" Ren asked after a few moments. Wasn't this what she was supposed to do? Create an impression of herself on the ice door?

"Can you pull your hand back?" Dali said quietly.

Ren felt her stomach hit the bottom of the deck.

Of course she could. Couldn't she?

Ren tried to lift her hand from the door. Her muscles strained.

Crap. Her hand was trapped. How was the ice doing that? The ice had crept back from the area immediately around her hand. Where was it holding her?

It took Ren a few moments to realize that the ice had actually merged with the sun that she was tricking into the door, twisting cruelly around it. The spears of ice trapped the heat, circling around it and encasing it, preventing it, and her, from escaping.

Though Ren tried to let go of the heat that she'd created, she couldn't. It had wrapped its way too firmly around her as well.

Ren shivered, but not from the cold. What the ice was doing was unnatural. It wasn't supposed to find an affinity for sunlight. No, it was supposed to shrink back.

But then again, this was chaotic magic. Maybe this was

one of the unexpected consequences: Changing the very nature of ice to make it heat seeking.

She studied the twisting spears. Was it possible to just break those apart? She tried, using her other hand, but realized quickly that her physical strength wasn't enough. She needed some sort of mental strength that she just didn't have.

Maybe she could put her other hand on the door? The first set of ice spears would release her one hand while reaching for the other.

Or at least that was the theory.

She realized her mistake as soon as she stuck her other palm on the cold door. The ice moved much more quickly than she'd anticipated. Not only did it not let go of her first hand, it immediately trapped her second hand.

Hmm. That wouldn't do.

When she looked over at Dali, he shrugged at her. "I'm not sure how to get you out," he said. "Not without hurting you."

Ren nodded. She was afraid that would be his answer. Not that he was opposed to hurting her. He'd do it as soon as she gave the word. Was possibly looking forward to it, based on his cruel smile. Maybe he thought that would teach her a lesson or something.

Better she do the damage herself, rather than allow him the privilege.

"Brace yourself," she said, giving him the barest of warnings before she let loose with the winds she'd felt lurking around her.

A howling startled her as hot air blasted the door.

The door shook. The boat wobbled. Ren thought she heard Dali exclaim, "Wait!"

But it was too late.

Ren's out-of-control winds shattered the door. Ice shards flew through the air.

As did Ren. She was blasted off the raft and thrown into the deep waters of the bay.

# SIXTEEN

THE COOL WATERS felt so good to Ren's sunbaked and ice-torn skin. Her palms throbbed with pain, prickles soothed by the water.

Ren opened her eyes and glanced up. Her head was still underwater. She wasn't in a panic, however. She knew how to swim.

And evidently, had at some point gained the ability to breathe underwater.

Huh.

Slowly, Ren rose through the greenish water up to the surface. She hadn't been unconscious when she hit the water. Not really. But she hadn't really been herself either. No, she'd been something in between.

With her first deep breath of air, Ren returned to herself. She knew that if she went back under the water, she would no longer be able to breathe.

Could she do that again? Or had it just been another unexpected consequence of dabbling with chaos magic? She couldn't say for certain.

Dali still stood on the raft, calling her name, looking out

over the side. He looked gratifyingly worried. There was no sign of the door he'd sketched. Her paddle hovered at the end of the boat. Though it wasn't touching the water, Ren could tell that it was acting as an anchor, holding the raft in place.

Ren waved her arm and called out to Dali.

He didn't hear her. He continued to call her name, moving to the far side of the raft and looking away from her now.

No matter. Ren was a very strong swimmer. She started swimming back to the raft.

After she'd been swimming for a few moments, she stopped and looked. The raft should be close, now.

Well, crap. It was further away.

Ren dove back under the waves and swam in earnest, wanting to yell at Dali for moving the raft away from her.

When she looked again, the raft had stayed the exact same distance away.

Unease filled Ren. There was some sort of magic going on, something she didn't understand.

She tried shouting again, but it was obvious that Dali couldn't hear her. She couldn't swim any closer. She didn't have any magic that could reach him.

She did, however, have a very loud whistle. It was in the top pocket of her jumpsuit, provided by the company for just this sort of emergency. A piercing whistle might attract the attention of someone when a shout wouldn't carry.

Ren pulled the whistle out of her pocket and blew into it as hard as she could. The sound pierced through the fog that appeared to still fill her ears.

Dali seemed to have heard that, at least. His head lifted and he looked around, though he still wasn't looking in her direction.

Ren tried whistling again, but Dali obviously didn't hear it clearly, as he couldn't seem to place the sound.

Was the raft still surrounded by a protection bubble? It must be. Probably the only reason Ren could actually see the raft was because it was *her* raft, despite how the company merely rented it to her. But until Dali dropped the bubble, she would never be able to approach it.

Calling out again wouldn't help. Dali wouldn't be able to hear her.

She whistled for a third time, then realized that the sound was going across the water on a faint wind.

What would happen if Ren used her magic to push the sound over? Could she just tap a small wind and not blow Dali overboard?

Ren had to try. While she was pretty sure she could make it on her own power to the next island over, she didn't want to lose her raft.

"HEY!" Ren shouted as loudly as she could, pushing the word over to the raft.

Oops. Too much. The raft rocked hard in the water. Dali stumbled and nearly lost his balance. But he finally turned her direction.

She waved at him awkwardly, while still treading water.

Good! He saw her.

Dali opened his mouth, obviously calling to her over the water.

She shook her head at him. She couldn't hear his words.

Dali shouted some more.

Ren sighed and pointed her finger to her ear, then shook her head.

He finally understood the situation. Dali looked around curiously before he finally realized that the protective bubble around the raft was holding her away, as well as deflecting his words back to him.

Ren continued to tread water when Dali held up a hand, showing that he wanted her to wait.

He put his hands together, palm to palm, fingers spread wide. Then he used his hands like a knife, cutting a seam into the protective covering. Ren could actually see the rent in the air, like a black scratch on a photograph.

Carefully, Dali pried the edges of the covering apart, creating a hole. "See if you can approach the raft now," he said. His words were clear, but they carried the echo of a great distance with them.

Ren nodded, then started swimming, aiming directly for the raft.

It took her longer than she expected to finally reach the edge of it. Dali grimaced as he held open the bubble and Ren pulled herself up onto the raft, automatically using her magic to steady the boat as she clambered onboard.

Ren couldn't help but grin at Dali as she stood. She didn't shake herself like a wet dog, though she was tempted to. She did try to temper the winds that she used to whisk away the water, drying herself off.

Dali shook his head at her, then fixed the hole he'd cut through the protective bubble, pressing his hand against the seam to smooth it out.

When he finished, he resumed his disguise and went back to sitting on the chair Ren had set out for him.

Ren took the hint. As soon as she touched the paddle still floating off the back of the raft, it changed form, back to what she was familiar with, shorter and with the single blade at one end. There might have been a hint of Dali's magic still at its core, but Ren knew that with use, it would wear off.

"I'm glad we tried that out here," Dali said slowly. "It shows me that you have a tremendous amount of power."

Ren shrugged. She didn't, not really. It was just that the chaos magic and what she'd originally been taught were so explosive when they were smacked against one another.

"But I'm beginning to understand that you not only lack control, you might not be capable of it," Dali continued.

The words stung, though Ren recognized them as the truth. She wasn't some chosen one, suddenly full of abilities and learning far beyond her years. No, she was merely a messenger. She'd risen to the height of her power, at least that which she could control.

"So what's next?" Ren asked.

Dali sighed. "I'm not sure. Warlocks don't really have gathering places. It's too dangerous to congregate. However, I believe I might be able to contact one or more, ask if they have a solution."

"Don't," Ren said automatically. "I don't want someone else coming to test me."

Dali hesitated, then he nodded. "I will be discreet," he assured her.

She knew it wouldn't be enough. "Please. Don't." He didn't understand the danger that he'd be placing her in, if another warlock decided to come and "work" with her. Not that they'd necessarily hurt her, but the company was already suspicious enough.

"If that's what you truly wish," he said. "Humility indeed," he added after a few moments. "I really thought that it wouldn't be this difficult to teach you a few simple chaotic spells. To get you over to my side."

Ren grimaced. She understood that he felt that his side was right. She wasn't convinced, however, no matter how much more the chaotic magic might have suited her or soothed her soul.

"I will need to leave Jung Wa soon, before I wear out my brother's welcome," Dali said after a few moments.

"But you promised to help me fix Market Canal," Ren pointed out, unable to keep the bitterness out of her tone.

Dali couldn't hide how he flinched.

"You're right. I did," he said after a few moments. He gave the issue some thought.

"We will try once more to get to the bottom of the issue with Market Canal. Then, I must be gone. I won't put my life at risk, not even for you," he said after a few moments.

"Thank you," Ren said.

"Expect me as a client in a few days," Dali said, standing.

In the distance, Ren could just make out the main pier for New Hong Kong, where she intended to drop off her charge.

With a brilliant flash, Dali vanished. The sweet smell of smoke choked her, coating the back of her throat like burned sugar.

Why had he done that? Ren didn't know.

People stood at the end of the pier, gesturing for her to come toward them.

No, not people.

Security guards from *Huli* Transport.

They'd been expecting her to carry Dali to them.

What was she going to tell them?

Hopefully, the partial truth she had would suffice.

---

REN SHOWED off her bruised wrist, where Dali had gripped her. She talked of the explosion that had occurred when her powers had collided with his. How she'd been tossed off her boat. No, he hadn't been there when she'd swam back to it. How shaken she was by the entire encounter.

And all because of her haircut.

She let real anger into her tone when she told of that. How dare he assume that she was interested in him?

Fortunately, the head of the security squad was a woman named Sanchen, an older Anglo woman with riotous black curls and dark eyes that bore into Ren and tried to pierce through her careful lies.

However, Sanchen heard Ren's disdain, and shook her head at how stupid the warlock must be to think that Ren was going to fall into his arms the moment he gave her a smile!

It took a bit of effort, but eventually, Ren convinced the security people that she wasn't in cahoots with a chaos wizard, that she hadn't recognized him through his disguise, hadn't known that it was him until he'd thrown it off, halfway across the bay.

They'd been interviewing her in a room similar to the first one she'd been in, with the cold, sterile white walls and the extra filtered air purified to carry more cold than normal air. The five people questioning her finally left, asking for Ren to stay there for just a few more minutes.

Just Sanchen returned. She carried a small black box with her. It looked like a jewelry box, the kind that carried the very expensive pendants that Ren's mom sold.

But the box wasn't made of velvet. The blackness of it sucked at all the light in the room when Sanchen placed it on the table between them, then pushed it toward Ren.

"I want you to take this, wear it at all times," she said.

Ren opened the box. The pendant was gold, maybe two inches long but only a quarter inch square. Wavy characters were etched in black onto each side. Ren recognized them as the sorts of characters that wizards used to call up a portal.

The pendant stank of magic. Not the syrupy sweetness of the chaos magic, but the burnt toast smell of old men and hectic mornings.

"Why?" Ren asked, her throat gone as dry as if she was trying to eat bread with thick almond paste and no jam. "Don't you trust me?"

"It isn't you we don't trust," Sanchen assured her. "But

him. He's going to contact you again. This will help us track him."

Ren nodded slowly. She knew that she could blow out the magic in this piece just by touching it with the slight bit of chaos magic that she'd learned.

However, that would tell the security people that she was, in fact, working with the warlock. That she had the potential to become a chaos warlock as well.

Had the company predicted that? Was that in her charts as well? The private records just shared between managers? She couldn't ask Xiyi.

What else did the company know about her that it wasn't about to share with her?

Ren slowly picked the pendant up. It felt cold against her fingers, but it warmed quickly. It was made out of a lightweight metal. Still, it felt like a heavy chain as she put it around her neck.

"There," Sanchen said with a satisfied smile. "Now, you're protected. The next time the warlock contacts you, we'll be informed."

Ren forced herself to say, "Thank you," though now she had a different problem.

Namely, how to warn Dali off from contacting her?

## SEVENTEEN

Ren had no way of getting in touch with Dali, of warning him away from her. She had no contact number for him, no idea where he was actually staying. She'd picked him up from at least two different islands so far.

Unless, of course, she contacted his brother. Wang Guanki.

Would he continue to protect Dali? Or would he turn them both in?

Guanki had sent her to his brother, seemingly to offer her up as a possible apprentice. Dali hadn't wanted his brother to know that he'd taken him up on his offer, lying in his initial message to his brother.

However, Ren wasn't going to be Dali's apprentice. She'd proven that she wasn't worthy. So maybe it didn't matter if Guanki knew of their relationship.

Surely he already knew that his brother was capable of lying to him.

The next morning, Ren just showed up at Guanki's office building. She crossed the busy, sun-filled lobby as if she had every right to be there. Fortunately, the same serene receptionist worked the downstairs reception desk and appeared to recognize her.

Ren pulled out her pager and rattled off a package number. Business as usual. Nothing to see here.

The receptionist looked momentarily confused. "I don't have a package with that number," she said. "Could you read it again?"

Ren nodded and studiously studied her screen before carefully reading off the number again. Hopefully the receptionist wouldn't ask to see the message.

"Just a moment," she said with a calm smile. "Let me call up."

Ren swallowed hard and took a step back, ready to race out of the building if her bluff was called by someone upstairs.

"You are expected," the receptionist said after a moment, her serene smile returning.

Ren blinked, surprised. What did that mean?

Or did Guanki share the ability to see the future, as his twin claimed to?

Ren took the elevator up, standing at the back and enjoying the way New Hong Kong shrank as they shot up into the sky. Summer hadn't yet started in earnest—a few clouds still dared to trail in wisps across the deep blue sky. It had been very warm that morning, as well as muggy. Ren couldn't wait to get out of the city and its stillness and back out onto the water where there would be at least the hope of a breeze.

But she felt she owed Dali at least this much.

The male receptionist nodded at her as she came over. He was speaking with someone else on his headset. He indicated the door beside him, which led to the familiar conference room.

Though Ren had expected that she'd have to wait,

Guanki was already standing at the far end of the room, looking out over the city. His black suit faintly glimmered with all the magic surrounding him.

What, was he expecting her to attack him or something?

"I had left a message that if someone showed up and asked for an unexpected package, that they should contact me," he told her with a sly smile as he turned to face her.

While it was difficult to tell the brothers apart physically, Ren had no doubt that she stood in front of Guanki. They felt completely different. Dali belonged out on the bay, surrounded by the waters. Guanki lived here, in the city, with the concrete and bustle. His spirit reflected that.

"Thank you," Ren said. She paused, considering her options. Then, with a nod, she pulled out the necklace she'd been given from Sanchen. She'd been wearing it under her uniform, as instructed.

While she knew that it would send out some sort of message if Dali came around, she didn't know if it would also record conversations. She didn't want to put Guanki at risk.

Guanki's eyes grew big. "I understand," he said slowly. He held up his hand so that Ren wouldn't say anything more while he thought.

A flash of magic went through the room. It wasn't the same protective bubble that Ren was used to. Instead, it felt as though Guanki had just filled the room with a morass of oil, everything sliding together and fluid.

"What you say now will be translated into something else," Guanki told her. His words had a weird taint to them, as if he spoke through a muddy well.

Ren nodded, though the action felt strange, slowed down. "Dali has been in contact with me," she started.

Guanki nodded. "I know. I warned him to be more discreet." He sighed. "That isn't in his nature, though."

"Did you originally intend for me to become his apprentice?" Ren asked, curious.

Guanki bobbed his head from side to side. "Yes and no," he said after a few moments. "I had hoped that given your solid nature, you might be able to tame my brother. Provide a steady influence for him. Even if you were both involved in magic of a chaotic nature."

Ren blinked, surprised by his honesty. "It isn't working out," she said, coming straight to the point. "I'm not able to learn from him, not how he wants."

She wasn't sure how much she should go into her own deficiencies. She didn't want to lay her soul bare before this man, but she would if it would help protect Dali.

"I see," Guanki said, though the expression on his face remained confused. "Then why are you here?"

Ren picked up the necklace again. "Dali is helping me get to the bottom of why Market Canal is being killed," she said. "I don't want him to blunder into some sort of trap."

"I will try to get a message to him," Guanki said slowly. Then he peered at her curiously. "That was you?" Guanki said. At Ren's confused look, he continued. "The ones who destroyed the monitoring equipment. They knew it was wild magic that did it."

"Dali did it," Ren said. "The canal is dead and the equipment lies about its condition."

Guanki sighed. "Something that big comes from the top," he said. "Start there."

"Can you help?" Ren asked. If Dali could no longer help her, maybe his brother could.

The dead waters were just wrong. Surely Guanki would see that as well.

Guanki hesitated. "I can make some inquiries, but I cannot guarantee anything." He paused, then added, "Good luck."

The weird echoes drained from the room and Guanki handed Ren a package that she hadn't seen earlier. It wasn't very big, maybe six inches on a side, covered in two layers of plain brown wrapping paper. It carried a small weight at the very center of it, but it wasn't that heavy.

"Thank you for seeing to this personally," Guanki said. "I really appreciate it. All the tracking information should be accurate now."

Ren nodded and took the package, knowing that a number had now been assigned to the box and entered correctly into the *Huli* system in retrospect.

It didn't matter where the package was going. Guanki was covering for her, pretending that he'd called her personally to deliver it.

"Thank you for your continued patronage, sir," Ren said formally. She took the package and bowed her head before leaving the office.

It wasn't until Ren got to the street that she looked at the address. She nearly giggled when she saw that she was expected to deliver this package to a postal service. A secondary label would be applied then, and it would be mailed to whoever was expecting it. She'd had other clients use this service, to misdirect the tracking of a package.

Ah well. At least it was better than having to go through a wizard's portal again.

---

THE DAY HAD STAYED hot and humid. Ren had just dropped off her last passenger at the public pier for Landao, one of the more residential islands. The feeling of the mass of people living there repelled Ren as much as some of the more dense neighborhoods of the mainland. She was looking forward to being finished for the day, to finding her own quiet on the houseboat.

Ren sighed when she saw Dali waving to her at the end of the pier. She was hot, tired, and really didn't want to deal with any more people. She longed for a cool shower and time to just stare across the water.

She didn't turn around and just leave, though. She waited for Dali to make his way to the end of the pier. He studied her for a moment, then nodded.

Again, that oily feeling surrounded her. The sound of the waves softly striking the pier overlapped and slid into each other. A seagull cawed in the distance, its raucousness muted.

"Bring nice clothes with you tomorrow," Dali warned her. "We have an appointment with Bi Qan, one of the directors of Mutashimo Electronic Works. Ten AM. I will meet you in the lobby of their corporate offices."

Ren gulped. At some level, she hadn't expected that Dali would keep his word, that after her meeting with Guanki, the chaos warlock would just leave the planet and she'd never see him again.

She nodded when she realized that he was expecting a response from her.

Dali spun on his heels and walked smartly down the pier. The oily feeling receded with him.

Did she have the finesse necessary to talk with a factory director? Was he or she the one responsible for Market Canal? Or was this person just the easiest target Dali could reach? Or had his brother helped, making the introduction for them?

Ren still had more questions than answers. Hopefully, though, the morning would bring some sort of resolution.

REN'S PAGER binged before she reached the sanctity of the houseboat. With a sigh, Ren pulled it out. Another transport or passenger that she'd have to deal with. That was just the way her day was going.

However, it was from her post office. She had a package.

It couldn't be the same package that she'd delivered for Guanki earlier that day, could it?

Despite her exhaustion, Ren went to the post office to pick up her package before heading home.

The small box looked the same as the first one, about six inches on a side. It felt the same as well, a solid something sitting in the center of a lot of packaging.

Ren waited to open the box until she got back to her bedroom. Inside sat a small glass jar with a white lid on it. The label on the side was hand-lettered with the single word, "Concealer."

When Ren opened the jar, the smell of magic wafted up, soft like a summer morning breeze, carrying the smell of rosemary and jasmine. The jar itself was filled with a brownish gel that felt smooth when Ren rubbed it between her fingers. She tried a small bit of it on the back of her hand.

Instantly, the wind-roughened skin smoothed out and turned a much more pale color. It wasn't until Ren tried to wash it off that she realized that while the change wasn't permanent, she wouldn't have to reapply the concealer very often. In fact, a jar like this would allow her to transform herself, her face, for months. Possibly as much as a year.

Ren fumed as she scrubbed at her hands. It took quite a while for the effect to start to fade.

She knew that Guanki had meant it as a kind gesture. He'd mistaken her nature due to her hair cut, the birthmark that nothing could change.

She didn't know how much something like the jar in her

hand cost, but she suspected it would be more than she made in a year. She wouldn't be able to afford something like this unless she was making a wizard's salary.

She was merely a messenger. She'd never make enough.

Still, it gave her a disguise for the meeting tomorrow.

And maybe something to consider in the future.

# EIGHTEEN

Ren studied her face carefully in the mirror. She recognized herself still, even with clear skin, her birthmark hidden. She'd rubbed the concealer into her forehead, along her jaw, even her clear cheek, making all of her skin the same consistent pale color, fading out the tan she'd acquired from being outside all day for so many years. Then she did the same with her hands, changing them from a worker's hands into something softer.

She wasn't delicate. She never would be. Her hands were still large, along with her shoulders and hips. She wasn't willowy like a model. She was strong and capable.

The main difference was that now she looked like everyone else on this planet.

She straightened the collar on her pretty white with black polka-dots blouse that she'd bought that morning. It suited her. She wore a pale pink lipstick and had used eyeliner around her eyes to make them stand out. Her skirt was gray with very subtle white lines going through it. It was only when you looked closely that you could see it was a checkered pattern.

For most people, she knew that the dots and the checks wouldn't go together. She felt confident that they actually worked, especially for her and her height.

She didn't bother wearing any sort of heels. That was a bridge too far. She'd never be able to pull those off. But she did wear pretty black slippers that had the perfect amount of material covering her toes, so that instead of making her feet look like flippers they almost looked cute.

No one else was in the public bathroom. Still, Ren hurried, hoping that no one would notice her transformation from messenger to personal secretary for an important businessman.

Ren took a deep breath, then another. She could do this. Walk into the lion's den. Apply whatever finesse she needed to get this director to stop whatever it was that they were doing.

After another few moments, Ren shook her head at herself. Nope. She was never going to be ready.

She was just going to have to go ahead and do it anyway.

Ren left the restroom with her head held high. She'd stuffed her messenger jumpsuit into her overly large purse, yet another part of the entire outfit that she'd bought that morning. She couldn't return any of the clothes, but hopefully she'd find another occasion to wear them.

It was only a few blocks' walk to the Mutashimo Electronic Works headquarters. She'd been relieved to discover that the corporate offices were not located in the factory itself. It meant that she wouldn't actually have to walk into all that noise and chaos.

At least, not right away.

The lobby was wide open, done in cool grays and soft whites, but filled with dark red furniture, couches and chairs, scattered like islands across lightly colored water. Several people were seated in various areas, having earnest conversations together. Ren recognized the white noise being washed through the area, in an attempt to keep the conversations private as well as to keep the area quiet. They were only vaguely successful, as Ren just heard the annoying hiss of the machines and didn't experience the effects at all.

Or maybe the noise was there to keep people from staying too long in the lobby, to encourage them to go talk someplace else.

Dali was impatiently looking at his watch when she came through the door. He wore a light blue suit today, with a darker gray shirt and golden tie. He wasn't hiding his magical status, as the red tie pin practically glowed with power.

Ren hurried over to him. "Sorry, sir," she said as she came up. "The bus was late."

Dali looked at her, then looked again.

Ren lifted her face to him proudly. She wore glittering red hairpins to keep the longer side of her hair in place. It made her very different haircut look stylish.

Who knew? Maybe she'd start a fashion trend.

"I see," Dali said, looking her up and down. Then he nodded and gave her a quick smile, obviously approving of her look for the day.

The receptionist called a name that Ren didn't recognize. Dali looked up, an arrogant expression coming over his face as he strode up to the desk.

"Wung Bi Qan will see you now," the receptionist said smoothly. She indicated the elevator they were to take.

Ren gulped as she stepped into the tiny, closed-off box. The hum of the electronics made her shiver, the feeling of ants already starting.

Dali reached out a hand, then hesitated. "You should straighten your necklace," he said quietly.

Ren was puzzled for a moment—she was wearing the

piece that Sanchen gave her under the blouse. No one could see it.

Then she realized that Dali wanted to "fix" it. She nodded and pulled it out, showing it to him.

He reached out and touched it, chanting a quiet incantation. Cold ice shot all the way along the chain around her neck. She shivered when she tucked it back under her blouse.

The ice wasn't going away anytime soon.

"If they are actively monitoring you, they'll think that you got the necklace wet this morning," Dali said. He gave her a huge grin. "Stupid of them, really, to give a messenger who works on a raft a piece that is affected by water." He turned more serious. "If the ice starts melting, let me know. If you can't tell me directly, ask me if I want an iced drink or something."

Ren nodded. She doubted that the necklace actually would stop working if it was wet; however, it was a good lie to tell the security people when, not if, they asked her about it.

The receptionist waiting on the top floor smiled at Dali and gave Ren a sniff of disapproval.

What, was Ren not good enough for such an Important Man?

Ren let her gaze wander over the secretary. Obviously paid well. Well educated, Ren would bet. Possibly had hopes of working her way up, maybe being appointed assistant or something.

But her shoes were old, and didn't exactly match her outfit. Ren let her eyes linger there for a moment before giving the woman a bland smile.

Though Ren herself was in flats, the woman stiffened, as if Ren had figured out her one shame.

She politely led them to a closed-in conference room,

with no windows. The table was made out of a hardy woodgrain plastic, shiny and heavy, supposedly expensive, but it looked cheap. The chairs were marvels of engineering, designed to support your back as you sat through interminable meetings. Ren wasn't looking forward to spending even a minute in them. The carpet was the same deep red as the furniture in the lobby, some sort of consistent theme for the company? The walls were industrial gray, cold and impersonal.

After serving them what turned out to be a very nice hot green tea, the secretary left and Bi Qan came in.

He turned out to be an older man, heavyset, with his hair buzzed spacer short. Did he have to travel off world sometime? Like most manufacturing planets, Jung Wa created all necessary parts on world, and assembled them into spacecraft off world.

Bi Qan walked stiffly, as if he'd suffered an injury in his youth that he'd never recovered from. He wore a heavy black suit that seemed more appropriate for the winter rains than the summer heat and humidity. Or perhaps it was just another sign of his wealth, that he never left the brutal air conditioning the office seemed to prefer.

And he had no magical ability in the slightest.

This would make things a touch more difficult. If he was truly mundane, not only would he not be able to see anything magical around him, no spell would work on him.

Ren had heard factory workers boasting of being as mundane as the directors. Was that one of the criteria for choosing a director? So they couldn't be influenced by magic?

Dali stood as Bi Qan came in, as did Ren. He introduced himself using a name that Ren had never heard of before, as well as giving Ren a new name.

Luomo, which meant flawless.

Had he given that to her as a joke? To cruelly remind her of all her flaws?

It seemed appropriate though, for a serious attendant to an Important Man. Not quite a princess name, but close.

The two men asked each other cautious questions about their health, their plans for their day off. It took Ren a few moments to realize that they were seeking common ground, something they could talk about.

It turned out that Bi Qan had a very fancy boat that he liked to spend time on. Dali appeared knowledgeable about such craft, and they talked engine speeds and hull sizes and weights.

Eventually, the tea quaffed and refilled, the necessary polite protocols fulfilled, Bi Qan asked, "So how may I assist a representative from *Huli* Transport this morning?"

Ren nodded in appreciation, though she hadn't realized that was the role that Dali was playing. It made sense. Only a powerful manager from *Huli* Transport would be considered important enough for someone like Bi Qan to agree to a meeting.

"I am responsible for one of the important water transportation divisions of *Huli*," Dali said. He appeared to be speaking slowly, choosing his words carefully. "There have been some reports about the quality of the water in certain areas."

Bi Qan's eyes grew wide with surprise. "Really?" he said. "Tell me more."

Ren shifted her gaze from Bi Qan to the cheap grain of the table. She reviewed the way he'd said his words, calling on her messenger training, repeating them to herself with the exact same intonation.

He was lying. There was a hitch in his voice that gave him away. Most people wouldn't have been able to hear it. But she did.

Had Dali?

"As you may or may not know, our messengers receive both magical as well as practical training," Dali said. "They're capable of piloting every watercraft available, as well as sensing things that are out of the ordinary."

"Do tell," Bi Qan said, his smile staying firm.

"The area in question—" Dali started.

"Market Canal," Ren said, breaking in.

Dali shot her a questioning look.

Ren nodded, all the while shouting in her head, *This is the one!*

"Market Canal," Dali repeated, sounding much more confident, "has issues. The waters aren't as supportive as they should be."

"What does that even mean?" Bi Qan said with a laugh. "I've worked with some of your messengers before," he said with a wave of his hand, dismissing the lot of them. "They are, as you said, overly sensitive."

Ren bristled. No, the rest of the messengers were *not*. There were very few who had her disabilities.

"And besides," Bi Qan continued. "There isn't anything that I can do about those waters. Mutashimo Electronic Works is *not* responsible."

Ren heard the warning in his voice. The factory already prepared to deny everything. Probably had bribes already in place.

"I see," Dali said. "And if *Huli* Transport disagrees? Or worse, the Seidaren?"

Bi Qan pressed his lips together in distaste. "Those blue idiots? They don't know anything either. Even less than magicians."

Ren blinked, surprised. She'd never heard anyone talk about the natives in such disparaging terms.

Dali gave the man a cruel, cold smile. "It would be a

shame if Mutashimo Electronic Works suddenly had to renegotiate all of their shipping contracts," he said smoothly.

Bi Qan grew quite still, as if he finally recognized the threat that sat in front of him.

"I see," he said after a moment. Then he shrugged. "We're not doing anything wrong. The waters are just going through a natural cycle." The way he smiled at them left a cold dagger in Ren's heart.

They'd bribed scientists as well, or just faked studies that showed that all the waters on this alien planet had a life cycle like plants, as if the dead waters could come back in the spring.

"That's your story?" Dali asked after a moment.

"Of course! Just ask the water council," Bi Qan said, his smile and confident demeanor returning.

"That isn't what the Seidaren will say," Ren said quietly.

Bi Qan snorted in derision at her. "Who cares what those creatures say? They're not important, not in the grand scheme of things."

Ren had never heard of such nonsense. Or such arrogance. The Seidaren hadn't invited the humans to Jung Wa. They merely tolerated their existence in the areas that the Seidaren didn't actually use. The contracts were renegotiated every year during the huge water festival of the Seidaren.

Which was going to occur the following week.

Tourists would pour into the planet over the next few days, everyone getting ready for the festival. Fireworks would be set off over the bay, and special tours of the Seidaren cities would be allowed.

Was this Bi Qan's goal? To somehow mess up those negotiations? To get the humans kicked off the planet?

Or worse, to think that the humans could arrogantly just take the planet from the natives? Maybe start a war?

Ren had heard enough. She knew that they wouldn't get anything else useful from Bi Qan.

Dali nodded, as if agreeing with her silent assessment. "And this is the official standing of Mutashimo Electronic Works?"

Bi Qan shrugged. "It is my understanding of how the world works," he said, glaring at Ren for having dared to mention the Seidaren.

"*Huli* Transport will be back in touch," Dali said, standing. "I'm going to go review contracts."

"I'll make sure that our lawyers reply," Bi Qan said, staying seated.

The two nodded at each other, a half-bow of the head, recognizing the other's power without acknowledging it.

Ren gave Bi Qan a cold smile and followed Dali out of the conference room, down the cramped, small elevator and out into the lobby. The heat from outside wrapped around them as they left the building. Despite how humid it was, Ren finally felt as though she could take a deep breath.

"The ice is melting," she warned as soon as she felt a trickle of water seep down between her breasts.

"Bi Qan is an idiot," Dali said sourly. "He's one of those 'human first' assholes."

Ren had heard of such a group, but she'd never had to deal with them before. "How do we stop him? Them?"

Dali shook his head. "Not me. You. I've far outstayed my welcome in this city."

Ren opened her mouth then shut it again. She knew there wasn't anything she could say in order to change his mind. Plus, he was right. He shouldn't risk his life staying here. And she shouldn't risk her employment by staying in touch with him.

"Good luck," Ren said. "Good journeys." She felt her mouth go dry as he gave her a quick smile.

"Thank you for understanding," he said. "Goodbye."

He gave her one last nod then strode off arrogantly down the street.

Would she ever see him again? Did it matter?

She'd discovered the source of the dead waters.

And there was nothing she could do to stop powerful men from doing stupid things.

PART THREE

# THE RULE OF FOOD

# NINETEEN

Three days later, Ren still had no clue what she should do about Bi Qan and Mutashimo Electronic Works. She doubted that the entire water council agreed with Bi Qan. Perhaps enough did, though, and they thought that causing a conflict with the Seidaren would convince enough people that they should go to war or something stupid. She didn't think that the humans were idiotic enough to go looking for any excuse.

Then again, she wasn't one of the Important People. Who knew what they really believed?

Ren was more busy than ever, not just with her regular clients and work, but also ferrying tourists around, as they bought tours offered by *Huli* Transport to take a ride on her "authentic" raft.

It seemed to her that there were more tourists this year. Every time she approached a public pier she found herself jockeying for a spot as far too many tourist boats were there. She also had many more near misses as she made her rounds: Some of the tourists rented speedboats and insisted on piloting themselves. They had no idea how to drive, or the rules of the water. If she could take this week off for vacation, she absolutely would. However she also made the most tips this week, as well as worked the most overtime.

One of the huge Seidaren cities floated closer to the mouth of Baohu Bay, to better accommodate the tours. Ren had always longed to take one herself—what would it be like to live on the water as they did? However, she never even got close to the city, as no one wanted to take a slow raft there, but instead wanted a fancy boat or even a hovercraft.

At least the early mornings were quieter. Ren relished her time paddling across the bay then, and its relative emptiness. The sun had already crested the waters that morning. The heat from the night before hadn't relinquished its hold. Her parents had actually started the air conditioning on the houseboat. No breezes would blow that day, except for the magical ones that Ren could use to cool herself.

One of the advantages of having worked with Dali was that Ren could now call up a single breeze, at least in the mornings when she was fresh. At the end of the day, she couldn't risk it, as it was much more likely to be a gale force wind that would knock both her and her passengers off the raft.

Still, even that little bit made her happy, as well as feel as if she had just a touch more control of her life, even if *Huli* Transport dictated her every move as well as her place in life.

She still wore the necklace that Sanchen had given her. Ren made certain to splash it with water at least once a day. Dali had been correct—when Sanchen had called her into the office, it turned out that the metal was reactive to water.

However, it wouldn't work unless Ren wore it against her skin. And there was no part of her skin that wouldn't get wet at some point during the day.

Stupid design. Arrogant people.

Hudie Dao rose up in front of her, her first ride that

morning. Though she was looking forward to her next ride with Hanshu, she knew that she was picking up someone else that morning. Or at least according to dispatch.

It surprised Ren when one of the Seidaren waved at her from the end of the pier. She'd rarely met any of the natives, and had only ferried one once before.

Then again, the last time had been the year before, at festival time.

Maybe the being also wanted to experience her "authentic" raft.

Ren pulled up to the pier and held the raft steady as the being floated themself down from pier and onto the raft. Like all of the Seidaren, the being was similar in appearance to a human, though was much smaller, maybe four feet tall. They had bluish-green skin and a broad face. Chubby cheeks bulged under their dark eyes, like an overstuffed child. Golden fuzz covered their head, the very center of it raised slightly, like the fauxhawk of a desperately cool teen. They wore a black vest that showed off their skinny, blue-green arms, along with a pair of tan trousers and plain straw sandals.

"Good morning," the alien said, bowing their head low after it had landed on the raft.

"Good morning," Ren said, bowing in return. "Would you care for a chair or a bench?"

The being tilted their head to the side, considering. "You sit?" they asked.

"No, sir, I will be standing here, piloting the raft," Ren said, taking her place.

The creature gave a cackling laugh. "Sir! Sir! How quaint!" they said. "Call me Gibbon," they said.

"I didn't mean any offense," Ren said hastily.

"No offense," Gibbon assured her. "Your name?"

"Ren," she said. She turned her attention to the raft,

calling up a slight bit of magic to get it turned around and headed back north, so she could get around the tip of the island and headed up to Man Dao, another of the islands that the Seidaren inhabited and humans weren't allowed.

When she glanced back at Gibbon, they had a curious expression on their face. "You use magic?"

"I do," Ren said. Surely Gibbon already knew that, right? Since they'd booked a ride on her raft?

"Interesting," Gibbon said. "Very different than mine. Show me, please."

Ren pushed the raft forward on a current. Gibbon giggled with delight.

"You give rides? All day?" Gibbon asked as Ren returned the raft to its normal sedate pace.

"I do," Ren said. "You can call the office and request my services any time," she added. It would be kind of cool if she had a Seidaren as a regular client.

Gibbon shook their head. Ren thought its expression had grown sad. "No, not here. Not live here. Visiting…family," they said after a moment.

Now their mouth twisted, as if Gibbon had just tasted something sour.

Ren heaved a heavy sigh in sympathy. "Family," she said knowingly.

"So many wishes!" Gibbon grumbled.

"I know!" Ren said. Her own family had been so surprised at her transformation, how the concealer had lightened her skin.

Mom expected her to maintain that normality, to look like everyone else all the time. Dad hadn't said anything but had looked thoughtful.

Ren was tempted to toss the concealer over the edge of the houseboat. Except, it was magic. And she didn't trust what would happen if it leaked out of its tight container and into the bay.

No, she'd just keep it on her desk, a steady, dark reminder of what might have been.

All the things that might have been.

"You see my magic?" Gibbon asked after a moment.

Ren wasn't exactly certain what the being meant, but she still nodded in agreement.

Gibbon gave her a happy smile and crouched down in the center of the raft. They started rapidly waving their hands back and forth. As they lifted them, a form started to take shape.

Ren watched the silent frantic conducting in awe. She wasn't sure exactly what she was seeing. But Gibbon was building what looked like a fragile tower. It was difficult to see the details, as it was somewhat transparent. It had a solid white base, then fluted pillars interposed with boxy shapes.

Was this what it felt like to be mundane? To almost see the magic occurring right under your nose? Ren had never experienced something like this before.

Just how different was the Seidaren magic? Could she not see it because of her lack of ability? Or was the alien magic just that, well, alien?

Gibbon gave her a bright smile when they finished. The tower was three feet tall, skinny and oddly shaped. "My home," Gibbon said proudly.

"It's beautiful!" Ren lied.

Gibbon at least didn't appear to hear the lie. "Is portal," they said after thinking a bit. "Can walk here, step, then be there."

Ren couldn't contain her gasp. "So I could go there?"

"You go there, yes," Gibbon said. Then their face took on a thoughtful look. "Sort of. I push, you pull."

Ren wasn't exactly what Gibbon meant. Still, it was

pretty cool to see the equivalent of a human portal. "Thank you for showing me your home," Ren said more formally, bowing to the being.

Gibbon paused, then added soberly, "Is safe. Not like *Huli* portals. No extras."

"Ah, very good," Ren said, nodding. No hitchhikers. Unlike the portals that the *Huli* wizards conjured. Being a messenger for the Seidaren probably wouldn't mean risking her life every trip.

Gibbon grinned at her and released the magic. The portal dissolved slowly. Instead of melting down into the ground, like a human portal, it evaporated, turning into motes of light and blowing away on unseen breezes.

Ren sniffed the air. The smell of baked, succulent fish came to her, a delicate scent that tickled the top of her throat.

"You go to Man Dao today?" Ren asked after a few moments of companionable silence.

"I do, I do," Gibbon said. Their smile trickled away. "More family."

"Go to mainland sometimes?" Ren said.

Gibbon wrinkled its nose at her. "Too many *beelanty*," they said. They waved their hand at her. "Humans. No water."

Ren couldn't help but smile. She felt the same way.

"You live there?" Gibbon asked, curious.

Ren rocked her head from side to side. "Houseboat," she said. At Gibbon's obvious confusion, she explained. "My home. On boat."

"Oh. Oh!" Gibbon said, looking excited. "On water!"

"On water," Ren said, nodding her head.

"On water is good. Is only way," Gibbon said. "Strong from water." They made a pulling motion with their hands, as if pulling something up from the depths.

"What if water is bad?" Ren said. She wanted to tell Gibbon about Market Canal. She wasn't sure how to communicate the issue though, particularly given the lack of a common tongue.

And whether this would be the start of the war if she did.

"Bad water?" Gibbon said, looking confused for a moment. "Ah! Bad water. No life." They looked sad for a moment. "Bad water, end of life. Seidaren need good water."

"Humans make bad water?" Ren said, trying to find her way through to the being.

"Humans make bad water," Gibbon confirmed. "Seidaren say no. Humans still do. Soon, no more humans."

"Ahh," Ren said. So the Seidaren were aware of the issue? That was all she could guess.

And they were going to kick the humans off the planet soon.

The humans wouldn't go. They would fight. Exotic minerals lay under the surface of Jung Wa, materials that humans hadn't found anywhere else. Normally, most mining was done out in space. Something about how the planet had formed, as well as traces of the Seidaren magic, made it unique.

Why was Gibbon telling her this? Was it well known among the Seidaren? It was the first time she'd heard of it, though. Wouldn't such a known conflict be on the news?

"Hanshu knows," Gibbon said after a few moments. "He said tell you."

Ren blinked, surprised. Of course, whoever or whatever Hanshu was, he'd know about this. Why couldn't he take care of it then? Why was he insisting that Ren deal with it? She didn't have any resources or connections! Dali was gone. Guanki wasn't about to help.

"Why?" Ren asked after a few moments. "Why me?"

Gibbon grinned at her. "Family," they said solemnly.

Ren had no idea what Gibbon meant. Her frustration must have shown, because Gibbon continued after a few moments. "You. Me. Raft. Waters. Hanshu. City," it said, point toward New Hong Kong. "City," they continued. "Family." Gibbon brought their hands up and intertwined their long fingers together.

Ren smiled and didn't roll her eyes, as much as she wanted to. They were not all one family. Important People like Bi Qan certainly didn't think so.

"There is…connection," Gibbon said after a short while. "Search deep."

Then the being pressed their lips together with their fingers and turned around, staring back out over the water.

Fine. Ren could take a hint. Gibbon was done talking with her.

But what good was a cryptic message? Particularly when Ren could use some serious help?

She didn't blast Gibbon with strong winds, knocking the being from her raft. But she sure thought about it.

The world was in serious trouble. Who was she to be able to fix it?

## TWENTY

Ren listened to her mom chatter as she made dinner that night. They sat in the kitchen, cool air blowing in from the air conditioning, making the room bearable. The earthy smell of rice from the cooker on the counter surrounded them. Mom had changed out of her good clothes and into a plain shirt and shorts, both in a lovely light blue that suited her.

Despite how tired Ren felt, her mind was still tripping over her problems, namely, how to stop a war. The news outlets had issued carefully worded reports of how the annual negotiations between the humans and the Seidaren were going. Though the official word was that everything was fine, most of the commentators agreed that, when they read between the lines, there was trouble.

No one knew what was causing it though.

How was Ren supposed to do anything about the negotiations? Or if there was a war, for that matter? It wasn't fair. She was on her own. She needed more help.

"And then this factory director came in, Bi Qan," Mom continued as she chopped up a pepper. She paused and looked over her shoulder at Ren. "Seems that someone in upper management of *Huli* Transport had recommended the shop to him. Do you know anything about that?"

Ren blinked, surprised. "No, I don't know anything about that. Who did you say came in again?"

"Bi Qan," Mom said. "He's a factory director. He was shopping for an anniversary gift for his wife. He was looking for a beautiful gold pendant that someone had told him about. Similar to the one you've been wearing," Mom continued slyly.

Ren hadn't been able to tell her parents where she'd gotten the necklace. They assumed that she must have a boyfriend that she wasn't telling them about. Then again, if any of their friends had seen her with Dali at some point, it would have been as good of an explanation as any, why she was with that man.

Ren slowly pulled her pendant out from under her T-shirt. She'd changed out of her uniform as soon as she'd gotten home that night, after taking a quick shower to wash the day off.

"I know you don't want to tell me who gave that to you," Mom said, coming over closer. "But if you could just tell me the store that it came from…"

Ren snorted. "It isn't completely mundane," she said after a few moments. "There's magic in it."

Mom gave her a bright smile. "Which means it's unique, right?"

Ren nodded. What would Sanchen and the security team say if she just gave the pendant away? Would it still work if it was touching the skin of someone completely mundane?

Slowly, Ren lifted the pendant from around her neck. It would serve Bi Qan right to be visited by *Huli* Transport security.

The problem was, would giving it away put her mom in danger?

Ren still handed the pendant over for her mom to inspect.

"Lighter than I expected," Mom said quietly. She held it up, examining it. "I like the characters etched on the sides of it."

Ren nodded. She certainly felt freer without that weight around her neck.

Had Dali gone to talk with Bi Qan in a different face? Had Guanki stepped in? Or had it been Hanshu? Ren didn't know, but she was grateful that she no longer had to wear that thing, even if it was just for a little while.

Though her mom didn't feel it, a rush of wind blew through the hot kitchen, as if someone had just opened a window. The hairs on the back of Ren's neck raised up.

The smell of something sweet came over her. Syrupy sweet. Like shaved ice drizzled with orange flavor.

"Take it," Ren said after a moment. She had no idea what Dali had just done to the pendant, but she assumed that it would be enough to burn it out, at least for a while.

Mom gave her a brilliant smile. "I will split the sale cost with you," she promised as she slipped the pendant into her pocket.

Ren nodded and gave her a smile back. It wouldn't be enough to get them off planet if a war started, but every little bit helped.

Where would they go? Ren could probably get a job as a messenger with *Huli* anywhere. However, then she'd have to be dealing with wizards and portals, putting her life at risk on a regular basis.

None of her options were good.

Dad came home late that night from his office. He worked as a manager for a printed advertisement company. While most ads were done electronically, there were still some companies who did print work. Dad constantly complained about the quality of the paper that he had to work with. The Seidaren required that it be one hundred percent bio-degradable, and not over decades but after a year. While it was good for the environment, and meant much less pollution, the paper wasn't as sturdy, nor the inks as reliable.

The weeks before the festival he'd had to work a lot of overtime, printing brochures and such that companies would use to target the tourists once they arrived. That night, one of the printers had broken (again) and Dad had had to stay while it was repaired.

"I've heard rumors that some of the other companies are cheating on the quality of their paper," he said as he helped himself to rice. "Thicker and less likely to jam or gum up the machines."

Ren nodded. Of course, people were going to try to get around the laws put down by the Seidaren. They were lazy that way. More concerned about today's profits.

"What's wrong, my beautiful girl?" Dad asked.

Ren looked up. She realized that she'd gone quiet and that both of her parents were now staring at her.

"What if the Seidaren find out? And decide they don't want to put up with our breaking of the rules anymore?" Ren asked. "What if they decide to kick us off the planet?"

"They wouldn't do that," Dad assured her.

"Why not? If we're poisoning their waters as well as their land?" Ren persisted.

Dad looked thoughtful for a moment. "They need us for space travel," he said slowly.

"How many of the Seidaren actually ever leave this planet? They need the waters here, don't they?" Ren said.

"You've been watching the news about the negotiations," Mom said after a moment. She continued before Ren said anything. "While I know that there's been talk that the negotiations haven't been going as well as they have previous years, that doesn't mean they'll completely break down. The company will fix it."

Ren tilted her head to the side. She'd heard that expression all her life, that the company would fix whatever was broken. As she herself worked for that particular company, she didn't have as much faith in it as others appeared to.

"And if they can't?" Ren said slowly. She wondered for a moment if *she* would be considered the company by her parents, since Hanshu had thought that she could do the job.

"They will," Mom said firmly. "Don't you worry about it."

Ren nodded but stayed silent.

*Huli* Transport did not allow wars on planets. But what if it wasn't between two competing groups of humans? What if the company had decided that maybe it was better if the aliens were removed from Jung Wa?

---

LATER THAT NIGHT, Ren sat at her desk, a piece of beautiful green paper sitting before her. She'd been thinking about how to recreate the tower that Gibbon had showed her. It would be boxy and yet fluid. The folds would have to start with a solid base. She might have to make the final sculpture out of two pieces of paper.

She wasn't sure she had the patience that evening to invent a new form, though. So she pushed it to the side, sliding some of the other papers on her desk out of the way, and uncovering the card that Dali had flicked her way the first time they'd met.

She'd forgotten about the card. He'd called it her tip.

Ren caused the light in the room to brighten a little as she examined the unusual card. It felt thicker and heavier than regular paper. Maybe it was paper infused with plastic. Would it dissolve into nothing if she sprinkled water across it?

Or better yet, if she dripped sand across its face? Overwhelmed the river with earth?

The back had a stylized portrayal of two identical rivers flowing down, meeting at the middle.

If Ren was being fanciful, she could assume that the pattern actually represented the twin brothers, both coming from opposite directions but working toward a single, common goal.

She snorted at herself, the sound loud in the quiet of her room. No, those two were out for their own ends. Not working together at all, even if Guanki had sent Ren to see his brother.

The front still showed a figure that looked like a stylized Seidaren. Since Ren had seen Gibbon just a few days before, she could see the details that were wrong. Not only were the colors off, the golden fuzz that covered Gibbon's head wasn't as solid as what was portrayed.

A brilliant green jumping frog was at the feet of the figure. A flowing river crossed the background of the card.

Ren hooked the long side of her hair back behind her ear and brought the card closer to her face. She could practically see the way the river flowed, passing from left to right.

What did it mean? Where did the river go?

The world shifted. Despite the brighter lights, the edges of the room darkened. Cold shadows gathered, pushing at her.

Ren felt herself falling into the card, traveling along the river. It felt to her as if she was back in River World, floating on her raft, carried by a swift current.

Only instead of the old American west building, the river

flowed toward a large concrete structure. It shot up in size until it towered over Ren, who still glided on the river.

Mutashimo Electronic Works. The factory.

Ren blinked her eyes and shook her head. Suddenly, she was back in her own room again.

She hated what the card had just told her. Hated it with every fiber of her being.

Yet, somehow, she knew that she'd just been granted a vision of the future.

She *had* to brave the floor of the factory itself. Maybe she could withstand the onslaught of the noise and electronics long enough to find out what was causing the waters in the canal to die.

Or maybe going to the factory would just kill her, and the card was predicting the absolute end of her journey.

It didn't matter. Ren was still going to sneak onto the factory floor, somehow.

Or die trying.

# TWENTY-ONE

It was easier for Ren to get into the factory than she'd imagined it would be. Masses of workers entered the building at the shift changes. No one actually checked their ID as they entered, despite the fact that Mutashimo Electronic Works dealt with sensitive materials, in particular the minerals found only on Jung Wa.

Was that fact part of why Bi Qan had so much disdain for the Seidaren? Did he feel as though he was paying the natives too much for mined materials?

This portion of the factory didn't have clean rooms, which was necessary for some of the more delicate electronics. Maybe those parts would be better guarded.

For Ren to enter, she just had to look like the rest of them. Be like the rest of them. Dim and chatty.

She couldn't use the magical concealer. No, that would make her skin too perfect. Instead, poorly applied makeup would give her the right appearance.

Just a pitiable girl, doing her best to get by.

Factory apparel was easy to acquire as well. Most workers wore the same style jumpsuit as Ren. They all wore different colored scarves and colorful bows in order to differentiate themselves.

The hardest part for Ren was finding the time and getting away from her regular work. There wasn't going to be a breather for her, not while the festival was going on. And she had the sense that she couldn't wait. She had to find out what was going on now, before the week was over.

In the end, Ren decided to tell her parents that she just had to work really late one night, and then enter the factory as part of the evening shift.

She waited close to the entrance. She couldn't hide herself in darkness and step out of the shadows into the stream of people. She didn't have the magic. Not necessarily that it would have even worked on the others—every single factory worker who passed her seemed to be completely mundane.

Still, she bided her time, pretending to be having a conversation on her (dead) communication device as people passed her by, waiting until the crowd swelled before she jumped into the current.

It wasn't that she was delaying the inevitable confrontation. No, she was just picking the perfect time, when she'd be the least noticeable. At least that was what she blamed her hesitance on.

The factory door was easily ten feet wide, and just as tall, as if at some point the designer had assumed some sort of mechanical transport going in and out of this entrance. The factory loomed like a huge, dark mass in front of Ren. Though bright lights shone just inside the door, she still thought of it as an angry shark, swallowing everything into its greedy gullet.

Conversations swirled around Ren as she stepped into the flow of people, the workers chatting happily about their families, their weekend, the coming festival fireworks.

Normal things. Not the end of the world or an impending war.

Ren matched pace with everyone else, her face down in an attempt to hide her cheek. She wore her hair pinned back under her cute green hat so that everyone could see her failure at hiding her disfigurement. It would repel people enough that she wasn't too worried. No one would look closely at her because of it. They might remember her, but she'd decided that was okay. They wouldn't know her face, just her strawberry mark.

It surprised Ren that the stinging mass of electronic haze didn't descend on her as soon as she entered the building. There was a haze of it, certainly. But for the most part, it seemed mild. Or at least mild enough that she could still think and not just run away.

Where should she go? The other workers all streamed off automatically, going down the various hallways. What part of the factory did she need to get to, in order to find what was happening with the canal waters?

Water. That was the key. Ren lifted her head and sniffed. Where was the water coming into the factory? Or more importantly, leaving?

There. To her left.

At least she wasn't the only worker going down that corridor.

The lights grew dimmer here, more orange. Or was that just Ren's reaction to the environment? Her skin started to buzz. The number of workers thinned as well, so that merely a dozen or so filled the hallway.

Ren looked around curiously. She felt the pulsing throb of huge machinery behind the walls on either side of her. The corridor itself was very industrial, with concrete floors and gray walls. The crowd she walked with passed several doors that she was certain were all locked.

Then the color of the paint on the right side changed to a very dark, familiar blue hue.

Wait a minute. How did she know that color? It took her a few more steps to place it.

It was the natural color of paint that was used to shield equipment and material from magic.

No wizards worked in the factory. No, they were all trained and then hired by *Huli* Transport. There wasn't much work for magic outside of the company.

Ren wished there weren't so many people around. She really wanted to be able to take a moment to send out her senses, see if she could detect what type of magic was going on behind those walls, despite the blue paint shielding the room.

Was it a wizard? Or was it a warlock?

Dali hadn't approved of the dead waters of Market Canal. Not anymore than she had, though his was from more of an ideological stance: there was chaos, then there was senseless destruction.

That didn't mean that all warlocks held the same opinion.

Ren wished she still had the pendant that she'd given her mom to sell to Bi Qan. The director had returned the next day and purchased the gift for his wife for quite a nice price. In the meanwhile, no one from security had come and arrested Ren for not following their explicit directions.

Though there weren't as many workers as there had been, Ren still followed along with them, noting where the walls changed color again. There were no open hallways off of the main one. She felt herded, though she hoped she wasn't being sent straight to the butchery.

Finally, the group spilled out into an open area. Huge hulking machines filled the space. The roof was at least three stories high, covered with search lights that made the room seem as bright as day. Each machine appeared to be a press of some sort. The workers would watch over the machinery, filling orders for electronic parts as they came in. While Mutashimo Electronic Works did normal parts, they also did customized machined parts for customers. This must be the room that fulfilled those orders.

The miasma of biting electronics fell like a torrent on Ren's head as soon as she stepped onto the factory floor. She forced herself to take a deep breath, then another. She could stand the pain for a short while. Then she was going to have to flee. Hopefully no one would question her leaving, particularly if she claimed she was sick.

At least there weren't that many people behind her. They were all able to flow around her, drifting to their stations.

Was there any water here? Ren fought against the blaze of pain that spiked behind her eyes. No.

The water was behind her. In those rooms where the magic was being performed.

Ren looked around. No one was paying attention to her. A few of the workers who were dribbling onto the factory floor glanced at her as they passed, but that was it.

Feeling great daring, Ren turned around and started walking against the flow, back up the hallway. Though her head still pounded with the residual headache, at least she didn't feel as though she needed to tear all her skin off to stop the ants from biting.

She returned to the section of the hallway where the walls had been painted blue. However, when she tried to send her senses through the wall, she found them impossible to penetrate.

Of course. That paint was supposed to repel magic.

However, whoever had done the job hadn't bothered painting the doors. Ren found she could slip her awareness through the gray door on her left in the middle of the hallway.

Water stood in the room beyond in great quantities. Maybe being kept in large barrels or something.

The door was locked, of course. Ren sent what she thought would be just a trickle of magic through the mechanism.

Smoke poured through the lock.

Oops. Too much.

At least that made it easier for Ren to open the door and slip inside, even if she couldn't lock it behind her.

Ren stepped into what looked like a mad scientist's lab. Bubbling water filled tubes that ran in clear swirling pipes above her head. Large vats were suspended around the edges of the room, the center taken up with bluish glass and conical caps of silver on either end. A control panel stood in the center of the space, like a conductor's podium.

Electric generators took up most of the far wall. Ren recognized them, as they were similar to the ones she'd seen at the head of the Munda River, though smaller in scale.

Ice picks jabbed Ren's right side, while the left side wasn't as bad. It took her a moment to realize that it wasn't the electronics doing it.

No, the water on the left was still alive. Vaguely.

The water on the right was completely, totally, dead.

These machines were a combination of both science and magic. They sucked the life out of the water flowing through the vats, then used that power to generate electricity. The factory was getting its power for free, as it were, the money meant to pay the utilities probably lining the pockets of Bi Qan instead.

An alarm sounded as Ren hurried across the room, heading toward the vats holding the dead water. Someone had detected her presence. Or maybe the broken door had reported its demise.

Ren found herself reaching for one of the tanks. The

water appeared to fizzle just on the other side of the glass, fighting to retain what vitality it could.

Could she bring the water back? Those were huge vats, each easily ten feet tall and three feet wide. It wouldn't require the *finesse* that a small amount of water would necessitate.

Plus, she really didn't care if she broke something. They were coming to get her anyway.

It was probably just her imagination that she heard someone shouting at her to stop, to not touch the water tank.

Ren pushed her hand against the cold glass. It was made of ice, like that door that Dali had conjured. There was *magic* here, of a chaotic nature. This had been created by a warlock.

It grabbed hold of her.

Sharp ice picks drove themselves into her palms. Spears of frozen cold wrapped around her arms. Her feet were suddenly encased in ice boots, holding her to the floor, entrapping her.

Ren shivered all the way to her soul and fought to pull away. She was as successful this time as she'd been the last time.

Were there guards now surrounding her? Ren wasn't certain. On the one hand, she was vaguely aware that someone was tugging on her arms, shouting at her, telling her to let go, to leave.

On the other hand, the ice commanded all her senses, frosting over her eyes, blocking her hearing. Even her sense of taste had turned blue, like the syrup from blue shaved ice.

The ice pulled hard at her, wanting her to fall into it. It wanted to entrap not just her body, but her very soul. Maybe even steal all her power once she floated in the dead waters.

Ren fought back the only way she knew how: by sending out a huge blast of magic that would destroy not only the giant vats in front of her but the ice and everything else in the room.

Hopefully, her parents would forgive her for killing so many of the security men and women surrounding her.

She tried to warn them away, tried to tell them to leave the room. All she managed was a desperate scream that turned all the lights to red, as if her eyeballs were already bleeding.

Then she struck with all her might.

## TWENTY-TWO

Ren walked carefully down the hospital hallway, one hand wrapped firmly around the monitoring station that she was still connected to. The walls had been painted a cheery yellow and many bright photographs of flowers were hung between the doors, as if those could distract anyone from the overwhelming scent of disinfectant and bleach.

It was quiet here, as this floor of the hospital was dedicated to healing magicians and wizards. The walls didn't buzz with electronics, and the lights seemed more natural.

While the medical doctors had rebuilt her broken body, a magical healer had repaired her magical powers. They'd "fixed" her, body and soul, so that she was no longer marked as she had been, and no longer as magically sensitive, either.

When Ren had first awoken, she was practically covered in bandages. Though that had only been three days before, Ren's medical doctors as well as the magical healer had wanted her to start moving. If she continued to heal well, she might be able to go home the next day.

Ren reached the end of the short hallway and turned

around, wheeling her monitoring station with her, like a boat dragging its anchor.

The room on her right had the door open with a news vid blaring about the latest developments regarding the accident.

Ren snorted quietly to herself and kept walking.

"Accident."

As if calling it that would take away the reality that Ren had deliberately blown up most of the ground floor of the Mutashimo Electronic Works factory, forcing hundreds of workers to accept unpaid leave for a couple of weeks while repairs were being made.

It had been an accident that several of the security guards who'd been trying to force her to leave the room had been killed in the blast. At least *Huli* Transport had announced that they'd pay triple the death benefits for those who'd died.

None of the blame had fallen on her. Ren still carried the guilt.

Others called her a hero for discovering the unsavory plot hatched between Bi Qan and his wife. They had been embezzling from the factory for years, shorting the payments to the Seidaren for the materials they received as well as no longer paying the huge electric bill.

Ren had watched the "thrilling" footage of the *Huli* Transport strike team descending on Bi Qan's wife, who, it turned out, was a warlock.

Draining the water of all life and power had had an unexpected consequence, namely, that not only was it impossible to revive, it also killed all the water surrounding it until it had been diluted enough.

Ren couldn't even imagine how shocked security must have been when Bi Qan's wife put on the necklace. Had it shorted it out immediately?

How had Dali known about Bi Qan's wife? He'd

suspected that there had been a warlock involved all along. Would Ren ever see him again?

Her breath caught as she saw a familiar looking man coming out of her room, his black suit glowing slightly from all the magic woven into the fabric.

No. That was Wang Guanki. The other brother.

As if he'd heard her, the manager stopped and turned around.

The smile he gave her did nothing to reassure her.

Still, Ren pushed on, determined to face him full on.

She stared at him with both her eyes, as her hair no longer fell over her face or covered her cheek.

When the surgeons had rebuilt her face, which had been ruined by the blast, they'd finally been able to remove her birthmark.

At first, she hadn't been certain whether she should thank them or curse them. Or perhaps both.

Now, Ren was able to look other people directly in the eye. Every time she did so filled her with an unfamiliar sense of power.

A look of uncertainty crossed Mr. Wang's face. It was so fleeting Ren wasn't sure if she'd imagined it or not. Then his smile softened and Ren knew he saw something more. Maybe a hint of what she could become.

His words filled her with dread. "Wung Meiren, I'm here as an official representative from *Huli* Transport. I'd like a few minutes of your time."

———

REN SAT in one of the two visitor chairs that were in her private room. Behind her a vent blew out sanitized air that was just above freezing. She had a blanket from her bed wrapped around her legs, and a second across her shoulders.

197

The window looked out on the peaceful courtyard of the hospital, a green area with wide walkways between the carefully planned trees and bushes.

The sterile nature of the view made Ren close the shades every time a nurse opened them.

Mr. Wang sat in the other chair. He'd ordered hot tea for the pair of them. They'd sat in silence drinking it. Ren wasn't sure what she had to say to the manager. He'd interfered in her life, assuming she was a warlock. Introduced her to his brother. Been the start of this long journey, which had ended in several deaths as well as her own much different place.

A wave of magic passed through the room, leaving behind a sticky residue. Ren suspected that whatever Mr. Wang said to her would be translated into perfectly innocuous chatter later.

"How are you?" Mr. Wang asked. It seemed odd that he'd ask that after so much silence.

"Recovering," Ren said truthfully. She wasn't certain what else he needed.

"Let's get the official business out of the way," Mr. Wang said. He told her of the benefits the company had paid her for hazardous duty, emphasizing that she didn't have to stay a messenger, that she could now change jobs whenever she wanted to, after giving appropriate notice.

As a declaration of freedom, it felt remarkably flat to Ren.

Did she want to be anything other than a messenger? What other opportunities did she have? She didn't want to work in an office or a cubicle. That was for certain.

As if reading her hesitancy, Mr. Wang said, "You could work as a personal assistant, you know."

Ren couldn't hold back her shudder.

Mr. Wang gave her a tight smile. "Think about it," he

urged. He hesitated, then said, "Do you have any other questions? About anything at all?"

"What happened to Dali?" she asked.

"I wish you two had been better suited," Mr. Wang admitted. "But he's gone. Off planet. At least for now. He'll be back to plague me during the New Year holidays, I'm sure."

Ren nodded. She wanted to ask about what would happen when their mother died, but it really wasn't any of her business. "And what happened to Bi Qan's wife? The other warlock?"

"*Huli* Transport does not tolerate warlocks. Particularly corrupt ones," he said sternly.

What did that make Dali? Someone who wasn't corrupt and could possibly be brought back into the fold? Was Mr. Wang actually that much of a fool?

Again, Ren wasn't going to ask. "And the negotiations with the Seidaren?"

Mr. Wang sighed. "*Huli* Transport does not support war in any form. Even between humans and aliens. It's bad for trade. Not everyone agrees with that, however."

"Who disagrees?" Ren said when he didn't continue.

"There are competitors to *Huli*, who would usurp us if they could," Mr. Wang admitted. "Rest assured, war has been averted. At least in the short term."

Ren gulped. It felt as though the temperature in the room had just dipped. "And in the long term?"

"Who knows? Who can actually see the future?" He winked at her. "We all know that those who claim they can are mere charlatans, right?"

Ren nodded and let go of the breath she hadn't realized that she'd been holding.

Maybe that was what actually held the brothers together.

Not their mother, but that the warlock would warn the manager about what was coming when appropriate.

As Dali had said, there was chaos, and then there was mindless destruction. Perhaps a war with the Seidaren fell into the latter category. Maybe that was one of the things that the brothers could actually agree on.

At least for now.

———

WHILE REN WAS in the hospital, she spent part of each night looking at herself in the mirror. All of her hair had been cut to about a quarter inch long. She could still see the red scars from her accident underneath the stubble. Her forehead was still broad and smooth. She hadn't noticed before how high her cheekbones were, or that while her mouth was small, her lips were not thin, but plump. Possibly even sensual. Her dark eyes held more wisdom than pain.

And her skin was clear. The mark that had scarred her since she was an infant was gone.

Ren couldn't just grow out her hair—that wasn't how magic worked. She did transform her face, making herself look as she had before, the blazing red mark on her cheek, her eyes haunted and hurt, her hair hanging down like a constant curtain, cutting off the world.

Then she banished the image.

No more.

She didn't have to go back to who she had always been.

Though she had no idea who she wanted to be next.

# TWENTY-THREE

REN PADDLED her way across the bay, enjoying the morning light and cool breezes. They wouldn't last for long that day, as summer now had its grip firmly on the world and wasn't about to let go for a few months.

She still worked for *Huli* Transport as a messenger, at least in the short term.

Everything was easier, now that her sensitivities had been dialed down. In the three weeks that she'd taken to heal after the explosion, she found that she could actually spend time exploring New Hong Kong now, trying new restaurants. She'd even made friends at the local noodle shop that she'd started frequenting, two other women her age who were also single.

Ren wasn't yet ready to leave her parents' houseboat, though she'd considered it. What would it be like to have a place on her own? She could afford it on her messenger salary, and wouldn't need roommates. But did she want to stay a messenger?

While she still didn't have great control when it came to her magic, she was starting to develop more. After Ren had been retested, Xiyi let her know that a new career path could possibly be open to her now, depending on her development: instructor.

Ren wasn't certain that she wanted to pursue that, but it was good to know that she finally had options beyond a strict office job.

This morning's client was one who'd asked for her specifically, though they hadn't left their name. Ren wasn't sure if it would be Dali, showing up out of nowhere, or if Hanshu was just playing games.

However, it was neither of them, but Gibbon who waved at her from the end of the pier on Hudie Dao.

"Good morning," Gibbon said after they'd jumped down onto her raft. They bowed their head to her.

Ren returned the bow, delighted that the Seidaren had remembered her, asked for her, though maybe it was still Hanshu pulling the strings.

"You look good," Gibbon commented, staring at her for a bit.

Ren didn't blush. She just nodded her head. Her hair was still short. Nothing blocked her face or her view of the world.

"You found, connection," Gibbon said as Ren turned the raft around. It took much less effort now to call up a touch of magic and send it across the waters.

"I did," Ren said. Though she hadn't used the *finesse* that Hanshu had requested. Not by blowing up the factory. Still, she'd gotten the results that had been needed.

Bi Qan and his wife hadn't been able to deny such a large explosion, or the investigation that had happened as a result.

"You still messenger?" Gibbon asked.

Ren thought it was kind of obvious that she still was. She responded with, "For now."

"Good, good," Gibbon said. The being smiled at her. "We need messenger," they said seriously.

"What do you mean?" Ren asked. Chicken-flesh danced across her shoulders as if a cool breeze had just caressed the back of her bare neck.

"The Seidaren. We talk with *Huli*. We want to hire messenger. From Seidaren to humans and to others." Gibbon paused. "Someone who understands connection." The being folded their long spindly fingers together for emphasis.

Ren didn't dare speak. Didn't dare ask.

Gibbon continued. "I give people your name. They say yes. You?"

Ren couldn't help but gasp. She wouldn't necessarily be paddling a raft anymore. But her position would be unique, at least at the start. She'd be *the* messenger to the aliens on Jung Wa.

While Ren didn't have the *finesse* that Hanshu had expected, she had something more important. The heart and the care to do the right thing. Maybe that would be enough. Hanshu had said that the fact that she cared about the dead water should have been enough to fix it. Maybe he had been right.

"I say yes," Ren finally replied when she realized that Gibbon was still waiting.

"Good, good," Gibbon said, grinning at her. "I show you more magic?" they asked.

"Please," Ren said, her eyes growing wide as worlds were created on her tiny raft, doors wide open and without ice.

THE END

## ABOUT THE AUTHOR

Leah Cutter writes page-turning fiction in exotic locations, such as a magical New Orleans, the ancient Orient, Hungary, the Oregon coast, rural Kentucky, Seattle, Minneapolis, and many others.

She writes literary, fantasy, mystery, science fiction, and horror fiction. Her short fiction has been published in magazines like *Alfred Hitchcock's Mystery Magazine* and *Talebones*, anthologies like Fiction River, and on the web. Her long fiction has been published both by New York publishers as well as small presses.

Find Leah's books on Knotted Road Press at (www.KnottedRoadPress.com)

Follow her blog at www.LeahCutter.com.

### Reviews

It's true. Reviews help me sell more books. If you've enjoyed this story, please consider leaving a review of it on your favorite site.

### Come someplace new…
Are you a traveler? Do you enjoy exploring strange new worlds, new cultures, new people?

Journey into the various lands envisioned by Leah Cutter.

Sign up for my newsletter and I'll start you on your travels with a free copy of my book, *The Island Sampler*.

I will never spam you or use your email for nefarious purposes. You can also unsubscribe at any time.

http://www.LeahCutter.com/newsletter/

## ABOUT KNOTTED ROAD PRESS

Knotted Road Press fiction specializes in dynamic writing set in mysterious, exotic locations.

Knotted Road Press non-fiction publishes autobiographies, business books, cookbooks, and how-to books with unique voices.

Knotted Road Press creates DRM-free ebooks as well as high-quality print books for readers around the world.

With authors in a variety of genres including literary, poetry, mystery, fantasy, and science fiction, Knotted Road Press has something for everyone.

Knotted Road Press
www.KnottedRoadPress.com